Julia Laughed....

a soft, silky laugh. "It's always been like that with David and me. Wherever he goes, whatever he does, I'll be right there beside him. We've both known from the first that that was the way it had to be."

Student Nurse Ann Galt, staring at the face of her lovely superior, heard the words and felt the shock of them, deep and numbing. She heard—but she wouldn't believe. How COULD she, when she knew that her future —and the fate of an entire island—hinged on one simple fact:

She must go back to live on that island as Dr. David Lochran's wife.

NURSE AT SPANISH CAY

Peggy Gaddis

PRESTIGE BOOKS
NEW YORK, NEW YORK

•

To my friend

ISOBEL JOHNSON,

With grateful appreciation
for her assistance

•

Prestige Books, Inc.
18 East 41st Street, New York, New York 10017

Chapter One

Ann Galt stood on the wide terrace overlooking the valley and saw, through a mist of tears she could not control, the beloved, familiar scene that she would leave the next day.

Below her the small village that housed the workers on the plantations that supported Spanish Cay were caught in the rays of the dying sun. The blue smoke of supper fires floated above them, scarcely disturbed by the sea wind from the Caribbean.

There it was below her: the village whose occupants were all friends of hers and whom she would sadly miss in the big, impersonal northern city to which she was going.

She was so absorbed in her thoughts that she was not aware of the approach of her great-grandmother until the old lady spoke.

"Ann dear," said Clarita softly. Ann turned swiftly, glad that the mist of tears had vanished from her eyes and that the smile, though tremulous, would not reveal she had been weeping.

"I was just saying goodbye to the valley, Clarita," she said with unconvincing gaiety.

"It's only for three years, darling," said Clarita gently, her eyes troubled by the obvious unhappiness of her beloved great-grandchild.

"*Only* three years!" Ann burst out, no longer able to contain the tears. "Clarita darling, it's a lifetime!"

Clarita, a slender, fragile-looking wisp of an old lady, her snowy hair partially concealed by the frail black lace of her mantilla, held high in the back in the traditional Spanish manner by an exquisitely wrought golden comb, smiled wistfully.

"How old are you, darling?" she asked gently.

"As if you didn't know!" Ann burst out. "I was eighteen in March. And now it's September."

Clarita, leaning on the stout ebony stick with its massive golden knob, sighed under her breath.

"And in June I was eighty," she said quietly. "And you speak of a lifetime as three years."

She settled herself wearily in a great peacock chair of rattan, and Ann came to kneel at her feet and to gather the frail, blue-veined old hands in her own. Her lovely face lifted to the older woman's.

"Darling, it's not that I mind being a nurse. I think it might even be rewarding. It's just that the thought of being away from the Cay for three whole years—" She choked on the words and could not finish.

"You'll have three weeks' vacation each year," Clarita pointed out. "There'll be only two such vacations, for when you're due for the third, you'll have your nurse's cap and your R.N. degree and you can come back to the Cay for good, unless you fall in love with some bright young doctor and decide to stay in the States."

"Phooey!" said Ann inelegantly. "Any bright young doctor *I* fall in love with had better have his mind made up to come back to the Cay and be our resident doctor, or I won't marry him!"

Clarita said frankly, with an air of making a long withheld confession, "I admit, darling, I had hoped something like that might happen when Dr. John began making arrangements for you to be accepted at that nursing school in Capitol City."

Ann grinned impishly. "And you thought I didn't know that? I could see it in every plan you and Dr. John were making. I'll do my best, I promise. If I can snag one before I finish my three years, can we come back right away?"

Clarita's eyes danced a little. "Provided he is a full-fledged doctor and licensed to practice anywhere in the country. We can't have a bungler here looking after our people. They have been faithful and devoted and we are responsible for them. That's why, now that your brother is gone, it's up to you to get the medical training that will keep our people safe."

Ann nodded soberly. "Poor Jerry! He wanted so much to be a really fine doctor, and he had only a couple of months to go before he would have finished his residency and been free to return. And then he had that beastly hunting accident! Oh, Clarita, it's all so unfair. There were others on that hunting trip who could have been spared much easier than Jerry."

Clarita's wrinkled old face that was like crumpled silk was heavy with a tragic look that reached to the faded dark brown of her eyes. She sighed as she touched Ann's shining blue-black curls and looked out over the valley where the short, swift twilight of the tropics was rapidly enfolding everything. She knew how it would hurt the girl to leave; she, herself, at eighty, doubted that she would have had the courage. She had come there as a bride at sixteen, and had been away only a few times before her husband's death; never since that time.

Behind them a footstep sounded, and a moment later a woman who was tall and spare, dressed in a neat dark dress and a white apron, her graying brown head capless, came out to them.

"Dinner is served, *señora,*" she said. "It's getting a bit chilly out here. Aren't you and Ann ready to come in?"

She smiled at Ann and added for her alone, "Tad is here."

"You promise me you'll take good care of her while I'm gone?" she demanded, her voice wobbling slightly.

"As I have always done, Ann dear," the woman, Tad's mother, answered. "You will find, honey, that the time will pass much faster than you think now. There will be things to see; places, people, fun and excitement. And you'll be back before you know it."

Ann nodded, her lovely young face grim.

"One year to a day from tomorrow I'll be back here for a three-week vacation," she said firmly. "It's in the brochure. It says that I can have a three weeks vacation every twelve months. Isn't that big of them?"

And because tears threatened and she didn't want to make Clarita feel too badly, she marched with her head high across the terrace and into the vast living room where Tad was waiting.

He was tall and rangy and sun-bronzed, so that his teeth made a white slash in his brown face when he smiled as he did now. But the smile did not quite reach to his troubled gray-blue eyes.

"Hi," he greeted her gently. "I'd give a couple of eyeteeth, pal, if I'd been smart enough to go away and study medicine when Jerry got killed, so you wouldn't have to leave the Cay."

Ann managed an unconvincing smile.

"Oh, you're plenty smart, but you're the mainstay of the Cay, Tad," she told him. "They couldn't get along here without you. Me, I'm just a very unimportant somebody. So now I've got to go away and become a fine nurse so I can take over for Dr. John. I will be one, too. I promise."

"Well, of course you will," Tad comforted her. "You've always done a swell job at anything you tackled."

"Thanks," said Ann grimly. "But this is the toughest thing I've ever tackled. To go away from the place I love best in all the world—"

"So that you can come back and look after the people who adore you—"

"And who have made a living for the Galts for two hundred years. Right you are, pal. Right you are," said Ann, and managed a deep smile as Tad's mother came in, moving slowly beside Clarita, offering an arm that would aid the frail old woman to move stiffly but safely.

A neat white-coated butler, his dark face like polished ebony above the starched white, bowed them into the massive dining room and began serving dinner. Afterwards, when they were back in the living room, Ann stood restlessly, declining the after-dinner coffee that Mary, Tad's mother, was offering.

"I think I'd like to go and say goodbye to Dr. John tonight," Ann said, and would not quite meet Clarita's troubled eyes. "He'll be busy making his rounds tomorrow when I leave, and I can't go away without saying goodbye after he's been so good about getting me accepted at the hospital."

"No, of course you can't, dear," Clarita agreed.

Tad stood up swiftly and gave Ann a heartening smile as he walked with her out of the room, leaving the two women to watch after them with pitying eyes.

"Am I a horrible old woman to demand that the child go away, Mary?" Clarita burst out as the sound of the jeep came back to them from the drive.

"Of course not, Clarita," answered Mary soothingly. "You are doing her a great kindness, though at the moment I imagine she doubts that. She has spent her whole life here, with tutors to give her lessons; a few trips to Port-au-Prince and Belize. Now you are sending her away to see what the world away from the Cay is like. She'll have a wonderful time."

"Unless she dies of homesickness," said Clarita sadly.

Mary laid a hand on Clarita's arm and answered gently, "Believe me, dear, Ann is much too tough-minded for that. And the nurse-training school will keep her much too busy to be homesick after the first few days. You mustn't worry about her, dear. She'll be just fine."

Clarita studied Mary curiously for a moment, and then she asked:

"Did you hope, as I did, Mary, that Tad and Ann would fall in love?"

Mary's color deepened.

"Did you hope that, too, *señora?*" she admitted her own hope quite frankly. "I'm afraid we were very foolish. After all, they have grown up here together like brother and sister. I think Ann feels that Tad is more her brother than Jerry was, because she has been with Tad so much more. Jerry was away for years taking his training, and Tad was here, learning from his father how to manage the Cay's industries. I'm afraid we were a couple of foolish old women to hope for such a solution as that."

Clarita eyed her with a vagrant twinkle.

"A couple of foolish old women, Mary?" she mocked. "I'm eighty; how old are you? Forty?"

Mary laughed. "I'm forty-three, as you very well know, *señora.*"

"And until now you've never called me Clarita. It's always *señora.* Why, I wonder, when you know that until you started only the natives called me the *señora,*" she wondered aloud.

"I never felt that it would be properly respectful for me to call you Clarita," Mary answered with the sturdy honesty that endeared her to Clarita. "Oh, I know you prefer it; but somehow, to me, it would have been very improper. So I taught Tad to call you that. And now I'm afraid you're stuck with it and with me."

Clarita put out her hand, and Mary accepted it and held it warmly in both her own while the two women smiled affectionately at each other.

"Then I'm the luckiest woman alive to be, as you call it, 'stuck' with you, no matter what you want to call me," said Clarita so earnestly that Mary felt the prick of tears behind her eyelids. "The day your husband brought you here to the Cay was a proud day for the Cay and for me."

"And for me, *señora*," said Mary quietly.

Meanwhile the jeep was traveling down the steep, twisting road that would have been impossible for any other vehicle to negotiate. Ann sat beside Tad, her hands folded in her lap, not aware that the tears were slipping down her cheeks until Tad glanced at her as they entered the village's one street.

"Hi, cut out the weeps, pal," he counseled as he brought the jeep to a halt. "After all, you're not going to be hanged. You're only going to a very fine city in the States, where you'll have a marvelous time and do things you could never do here on the Cay."

"Ha!" said Ann grumpily and contemptuously. "Why didn't you and I fall in love and get married, Tad? Then there wouldn't be any of this nonsense about me being sent into exile to learn to be a nurse."

"It was thoughtless of us, I guess," said Tad quite seriously. "But we grew up here together and have known each other since we were infants. It would be like falling in love with your own brother or sister. And now that Jerry's gone, the physical well-being of the people on the Cay must be considered. The *señora* had tried and tried to lure a doctor to come here. But she can't get a good one, and she won't have a bad one! So what else is to be done?"

"I'll only be a nurse; I won't be a doctor," Ann reminded him, and added ruefully, "Clarita is hoping I can snag some fine, upstanding young medic who'll fall head over heels in love with me and be willing to marry me and come down here to practice. Isn't that a laugh?"

Tad studied her intently in the light from the huge moon that was just heaving itself out of the sea, and said thoughtfully, "Well, now, I don't know. You shouldn't have *too* much trouble. You're a darned good-looking gal, Ann."

"Well, thanks heap," Ann told him, and tried hard to sound gay.

"Don't mention it," said Tad handsomely, and grinned at her.

"The only trouble with that solution is that if I found a doctor who fell in love with me and were willing to come down here and live, he'd probably have something wrong with him: a lack of ambition or of preparation for his job. There'd have to be some reason he'd be willing to set up shop in a place like the Cay, with no expensive fees to collect and no luxury patients to attend."

"That," Tad told her firmly, "is a very negative attitude and will get you nothing but disappointment. Here we are at the clinic. Dr. John's light is on in his office, so he's expecting us."

The climbed out of the jeep in front of the neat, square, white stucco-block building and walked across the small green velvet lawn with its border of blossoming hibiscus and oleanders. At the window they paused, stilled by what they could see through its well-polished glass.

A stout elderly man, his hair thick and white and uncombed, his giant white mustache hiding his slightly open mouth, sat asleep at the big old-fashioned mahogany desk. In shirt-sleeves, because the night was hot, with a giant fan rotating the still air above his head, he slept like a tired child.

Ann felt a swift stab of compunction. She had been grousing about having to give up three years on the Cay in order to relieve this worn, tired old man of his heavy responsibilities in taking care of the Cay's workers and their families. Yet Dr. John had given up a good practice, without a hint of regret, to come there nearly forty years ago; he had done research in tropical diseases, and attained some small measure of fame among his colleagues by papers he had written that had been published in medical journals. No one had ever heard one word of regret for his vanished States-side practice. He had devoted himself selflessly to the well-being of the Cay; and she, whose property the Cay would some day be, had felt resentful that she had to leave the place long enough to be trained to take his place when he could no longer handle the needs of the people.

She turned to Tad, and the moonlight revealed the shine of threatening tears in her eyes.

"I'm going to be the best darned nurse any training school ever turned out," she told him unsteadily. "I'm not going to let him or the Cay down!"

"Well, of course you're not," Tad told her softly, his arm about her, steadying her, as they turned toward the door. "You'll be a fine nurse, and the Cay will be well taken care of."

She gulped on a sob and managed a watery smile.

"Tad, dear, you're such a comfort!"

"Always glad to oblige, you goof!"

She hesitated a moment at the door.

"We mustn't let him know we found him taking a cat nap," she said softly. "Let's make some noise and wake him before we go in. He'd be so embarrassed if he thought we'd seen him asleep this early in the evening."

They crept back to the jeep. Tad slammed the door hard, and they both laughed loudly. Ann caught his arm, leaning against him a moment as she fought the tears that threatened, before they marched gaily and noisily up the shell-paved path to the door of the clinic and rapped on the door. Then they pushed it open and surged inside with gay shouts of greeting.

They found Dr. John still at his desk, very busy writing up a case history. He looked up at them over his spectacles as they came in.

"Well, well, look who's here," he greeted them with warm affection.

"You surely didn't think I'd go away without saying goodbye, Dr. John?" Ann asked accusingly, as she bent to lay her cheek for a moment against his.

"Oh, I was planning to be at the dock in the morning to see you off," he assured her.

"Provided you hadn't had a sudden call to the sugar mill where somebody had met a *fer-de-lance* face to face," Ann laughed; "or some farmer in the interior hadn't slashed himself with a machete while gathering bananas from his personally owned trees."

"Such emergencies don't happen often," Dr. John protested, and grinned at her fondly. "So tomorrow you're going off to the States to learn to be a nurse."

"Since you've been pulling strings and writing to your

old friends back at Blalock Memorial for the past year to get them to accept me as a student nurse, you can hardly be surprised," Ann said gaily.

Dr. John studied her for a moment, and then he sighed and shook his white head.

"Little Ann, that I spanked into life just a handful of years ago and now you're going to train for nursing in the hospital where I interned, more years ago than I care to remember," he mused aloud.

"Evidently a great many people at Blalock Memorial remember and are proud, and willing to grant you the favor of accepting a probationer like me just because you recommended me," she reminded him. "And I won't let you down, Dr. John. I'll work hard, and I'll behave, and I'll come back here a fine, dedicated nurse. And together you and I will make Spanish Cay the healthiest spot in the Caribbean. That's a promise, Dr. John. And you know I don't go back on my promises."

"Of course you don't, dear," said Dr. John gently. "You'll make a fine nurse. I've watched you when you've been helping me; that was one of the reasons I encouraged Clarita to prepare you for a nursing course. I saw to it that the tutors she got for you taught you the subjects most important for you to know when you face your examination at the training school."

Ann nodded soberly. "I'll be back for my three-week vacation at the end of my first year," she promised him gaily. "And then you can check on me and see if I've begun to learn the things you consider most important."

"Vada Marshall will attend to that," said Dr. John. "She's the superintendent of nurses; tough-minded, hard-boiled as such a woman has to be, but fair and impartial. You'll be frightened to death of her at first, but when you get to know her, you'll admire and respect her as everybody does who completes her training."

"You never mentioned her by name before, Dr. John," Ann said.

Dr. John's tired eyes took on a far-away look, and both Ann and Tad realized that he was lost in memories of that other world he had known before he had come to Spanish Cay.

"Was she a very close friend, Dr. John?" Ann probed gently.

Dr. John turned his eyes to her as though for a moment he had forgotten her presence.

"A close friend? Vada?" he asked. And Ann could have sworn there was a trace of heightened color in the old man's face. "Well, yes, you might say she was a close friend. I was an interne, fighting hard for a residency; she was a senior student nurse with a large family of brothers and sisters to provide for when she completed her training. So friends was about all we could hope to be. When I wrote to her about you, she remembered me."

"I'm glad," said Ann softly. "I'm very glad you told me, because now if she gets really tough, instead of being terrified I'll just look at her and think, 'You used to be a good friend of Dr. John's. And nobody who was ever a friend of Dr. John's could be all bad!' "

Dr. John laughed and heaved himself to his feet, and Ann's heart contracted a little as she saw the effort that took.

"And now let's all three have a drink, to toast your future and that of the Cay when you return," he suggested.

He brought out a squat brown bottle from the small refrigerator and poured three sizable glasses of iced papaya juice in which, quite solemnly, they drank the toast he had suggested.

Chapter Two

Forty-eight hours later Ann stood in the center of a room no larger than her dressing room at the Cay. Yet it held two single beds; a dresser with four drawers and a mirror above; a desk in a corner, and a wicker chair. That was all. And she was to share it with another girl. The two beds told her that.

She looked about her, and a wave of such bitter homesickness swept over her that it took all her strength to fight it down. Three whole years cooped up in this tiny clothes closet!

She opened the closet door and was thankful tha. she had brought only one suitcase with her, at Dr. John's suggestion. He had explained she would be wearing uniforms on duty; and on her off-duty hours she could shop in the stores of Capitol City, which, he assured her, were among the best in the country.

Her unhappy reverie was interrupted by the opening of the door, and she turned to face the girl who stood hesitantly there. The girl was older than herself, rather plain, with red hair and freckles and a slightly tip-tilted nose.

"Hello," she greeted Ann with tentative good fellowship. "I suppose we're going to be roomies. My name is Jessie Allen. What's yours?"

"Hello, Jessie. I'm Ann Galt."

"Where are you from, Ann?" asked Jessie, tested the bed nearest the door and looked pleased at its resiliency.

"From Spanish Cay," said Ann, and added as Jessie looked up at her, puzzled. "It's an island in the Caribbean between Haiti and Honduras."

"Well, forevermore!" gasped Jessie, saucer-eyed. "Who'd ever think I'd have the luck to get a roomie who had honestly *seen* the Caribbean!"

Ann felt some of her homesickness vanishing as she laughed and dropped down on the edge of her bed.

"I've not only seen it," she laughed. "I was born there and lived there all my life until forty-eight hours ago."

"Well, I never hoped to get a roomie who had seen some of those 'far-away places with the strange-sounding names,'" Jessie said in awed admiration. "Tell me about it. It must be a fabulous place."

"It is," said Ann softly. She closed her eyes and for a moment was back there, watching the lazy rolling surf break on the golden-yellow beach.

There was a light knock at the door, and both roommates turned as it opened to admit a girl whose uniform marked her as a senior student nurse.

"Hi, Probies," she greeted them gaily. And as Ann still sat on the side of her bed, the newcomer shook an admonitory finger at her. "Naughty, naughty, Probie! Don't you know that you're supposed to stand in the presence of a nurse senior to yourself?"

"Well, golly, everybody's senior to us," answered Ann, scarlet of cheek, as she scrambled to her feet.

"Right you are, my girl. Therefore expect to spend an awful lot of time on your feet for the next three years," laughed the newcomer, and there was warm friendliness in her eyes. "Of course next year you can make the probies stand when *you* enter a room."

"I don't think I'd like that," Ann burst out. "It sounds terribly snobbish if not downright arrogant."

"Oh, come now, surely you don't really believe that!" protested the newcomer. "You are supposed to stand in the presence of a nurse senior to yourself or of a doctor out of respect for his or her profession, not because of the man or woman. It is a mark of respect that is a convention, a tradition, a regulation of the medical profession. A nurse's first thought must be for her patient, and so must the doctor's. A nurse must respect a doctor's orders and obey them without question or hesitation as a soldier is expected to respect the orders of his superior officers. Now do you understand why you must stand when someone superior in training to you enters a room?"

"I'm sorry," Ann managed stiffly. "I do understand now."

The newcomer smiled and consulted a slip of paper she carried.

"Which of you is Ann Galt?" she asked.

"I am."

The newcomer looked at Jessie. "Then you're Jessie Allen."

"Yes, ma'am."

"I'm Julia Anderson, your Big Sister," she told them.

The two girls stared at her, wide-eyed, and it was Jessie who managed to ask faintly, "Our *what?*"

"Your Big Sister," Julia explained. "I'm supposed to watch over you like a mother-hen over her chicks; see that you get properly oriented. If you have problems you are supposed to bring them to me, and between us we are supposed to work them out. I want you to feel perfectly free to come to me any time something puzzles you about the routine, the hospital, the rules and regulations. And I warn you that for the first few months you'll be completely bewildered and constantly tripping over those rules and regulations. But I do want you to feel that for every rule and regulation you may stumble over, there's a good, sound reason. And when you understand that reason you'll be glad to obey."

She studied them both with her warm, friendly regard. Ann thought the shining chestnut brown hair beneath the tiny senior student cap was lovely. Julia's eyes were golden-brown, and her skin was smooth and faintly touched with the slightest and most deft make-up. Julia was, Ann decided, really a beauty, and she could only hope that when her time came to don that pale green uniform it would be as becoming to her as it was to Julia.

"Well, now, are there any more questions?" Julia asked lightly.

"Not for the present," Ann answered cautiously, and Jessie nodded a shy agreement.

"Fine. Then you'd better scamper down to the cafeteria and get your lunch. You're due in the sewing room for your uniforms to be fitted at half past two. And since we have a very large class of probies this term, I must ask you to be on time. I'll be around to guide you to the sewing room. 'Bye for now."

She went out and closed the door behind her, and for a moment the two girls left in the room just stared at the door and then at each other.

"A Big Sister yet!" murmured Jessie as she lifted her shabby suitcase to the bed and opened it. "They think of everything here, don't they?"

She was grinning impishly, and Ann asked curiously, "What are you chuckling about?"

"About suddenly acquiring a big sister when I've been a big sister to my whole brood of brothers and sisters ever since I can remember, almost," Jessie answered. "My father is a tenant farmer, and there is a houseful of kids. That's why I'm so late getting started in training. I'm twenty-two; and the preferred age is eighteen. But I had to wait until my kid sister, Margie, was old enough to take my place and be a big sister to the other kids. My mother is an invalid, and Pop doesn't make enough to pay a housekeeper. In fact, I'd never have made it here if some of the people at the church hadn't decided to give me a scholarship. I've promised to come back and be a county nurse when I've finished my training."

She spoke so matter of factly, while she was unpacking

the contents of her shabby suitcase, that Ann could only stare at her.

Holding a dark blue dress and matching jacket which she was arranging with loving care on a hanger, Jessie looked over her shoulder at Ann, her blue eyes twinkling.

"And now I've got a Big Sister of my own," she mocked. "My stars! I could tell her a few things about what that means! Only of course it won't mean the same thing here."

After hanging the dress, she turned back to face Ann.

"Isn't this a lovely room?" she said happily. "And just think: we have it all to ourselves!"

Ann blinked and looked once more about the tiny cubicle.

"It's very small, don't you think?" she asked uneasily.

Jessie's sandy eyebrows went up above honestly surprised blue eyes.

"For just the two of us?" she gasped. "My stars and bars, Ann, what do you want? Why, down home this would hold three or four people."

"By bulging at the seams?" asked Ann dryly.

Jessie said quietly, and now there was a faintly hostile gleam in her eyes, "I'm afraid, Ann, that you've been accustomed to a great deal more than I have, and if you feel you'd be happier rooming with someone closer to your own social position—"

Ann stared at her, shocked. "Why, Jessie, don't talk like a bloomin' idiot!" she protested. "My social position, my eye! Who do you think I am, anyway? A masquerading princess? I never heard of such rot! I'm tickled pink to have you as a roomie; and if I've hurt your feelings—"

"Stars and bars!" Apparently it was Jessie's favorite expletive. "We can't start out being sensitive and getting our feelings hurt! Of course you didn't, Ann. We're going to have to live together for three years, and it would be just too bad if we couldn't be friends, now, wouldn't it?"

Ann hugged her impulsively.

"Of course it would, Jessie," she said eagerly. "I guess I'm just a little bit homesick, that's all, and more than a little scared. Aren't you?"

Jessie grinned. "I'm either scared pea-green or else I'm hungry," she admitted. "If I'm scared, only time can cure that; but if I'm hungry, our Big Sister said there was plenty we could do about it. Where's that cafeteria Julia was telling us about?"

As they both moved toward the door, Jessie turned a scared face toward Ann.

"Oh, boy, I called her 'Julia,' " she remembered. "Maybe I should have said 'Miss Anderson,' or 'Your Majesty.' "

Ann laughed as she swung the door open.

"Now who ever heard of calling a Big Sister 'Your Majesty'?" she teased.

"Princess Margaret; who else?" Jessie laughed and led the way down the corridor and to the elevator.

They paused, abashed and bewildered at the clamorous noise that met them as they entered the cafeteria: a huge place that was crowded with tables. As they entered the serving line, Ann wondered if they would be able to find an unoccupied table. But when their trays were laden and they started away from the serving line, a hand touched Ann's arm lightly and they were motioned toward a large table at the side of the room where a dozen or more other probationers, still in their arrival clothes, sat. The moment they accepted the two vacant chairs and began unloading their trays, the cheerful babble of conversation from the other girls engulfed them. And by the time they were seated questions were flying back and forth, and a cheerful bubble of laughter had wiped out the scared, lonely feeling.

At a nearby table, unnoticed by either Ann or Jessie, Julia sat with a final cup of coffee and a cigarette, while David Lochran, in starched hospital whites, his name on a small tag applied to his lapel, finished his second helping of pie.

"There they are, Dave," Julia told him softly. "My two chicks."

"Which two?" asked David with friendly interest.

"The redhead with her back to us, and that delectable creature with the raven's wing hair and the impossibly perfect figure," Julia told him, still watching the girls. "The brunette is old Dr. John's protégé. Remember him?"

David nodded. "I never knew him, of course, but he's a sort of legend around here. The kid ought to make quite a nurse, if he's sponsoring her. Isn't he living in retirement somewhere down in the Caribbean?"

"He's resident doctor to the Galt plantation's several

hundred native workers at a place called Spanish Cay, where the girl was born and brought up," answered Julia. "Miss Marshall told me a lot about him when she found I'd drawn Ann's name as one of my pet charges."

"Who's the redhead?" asked David. "From here, she's cute as a button."

"That's Jessie Allen, whose church Christian Service Committee is sponsoring her on her promise to come back and serve as county nurse for at least a year after she graduates."

"I'd say you've picked yourself a couple of very interesting girls, Julie."

Julia laughed and lifted her shoulder in a pretense of a shrug.

"You know that's not the way the Big Sister Committee works," she reminded him lightly. "The names of all the probationers are dropped into a box and names are drawn. It was just luck I got them; but you know something? It's a very large class, and I'll bet there are a lot of interesting girls in it, and no Big Sister need be disappointed at the names of the ones she drew. I just hope we can all see them out of their pink uniforms and into student nurse blues by the end of the pre-clinical period."

David eyed her with warm admiration.

"I'll be on hand to see your two chicks get their candles lighted by you at the end of their pre-clin," he told her.

"You're a lamb, David. Thanks for your confidence."

"What the heck? How could they miss, with you standing by to offer assistance and encouragement and a pretty shoulder to weep on?" asked David as if there could not possibly be any doubt.

Julia felt a small warm glow about her heart. She and David had been good friends since their first meeting, when she had been a big-eyed, scared but hopeful first year student nurse and he had been a first year interne. Soon now they would both emerge from the chrysalis of their training: he as a full-fledged doctor with a year's residency behind him; she as an RN with a cherished cap and pin.

She stood up and said briskly, "Well, I've got to get back to the ward. See you all of a sudden one of these days, Davie m' boy. And I only hope I never forget to say humbly, 'Yes, Doctor,' when you speak to me in the presence of a superior."

"Superior in rank, honey; never in any other way," David assured her as he walked beside her out of the cafeteria and they parted in the corridor to go their separate ways in the busy round of their activities. As Julia hurried back to Pediatrics and her duty hours there, a small eager hope bloomed radiantly in her heart. David liked her, that was certain. And perhaps there was more than that.

Chapter Three

Ann had expected to be bitterly homesick in her first weeks at the training school. But she found, as she entered the preliminary eight weeks of classroom work, that she was so desperately tired when the day ended that she fell asleep almost before she was in bed. And after the eight weeks of classroom work, when she and the other probationers were given two to ten hours a week in the ward, putting into effect under the sharp-eyed supervision of faculty the things they had learned in class, she became so intensely interested in what she was doing that there was little time for any thought of a world that lay beyond the confines of the place.

She and Jessie had become fast friends. They had turned to Julia many times and had found her sturdy, steady common sense a great comfort. The days slid by so fast that she scarcely sensed the approach of Christmas until she saw the decorations beginning to go up in the wards and the huge tree that suddenly appeared in the day room.

"Golly," she gasped incredulously to Jessie, "it can't be Christmas."

"What makes you think so?" demanded Jessie, a wistful look in her blue eyes. "I bet the stores down home have had their decorations up since Hallowe'en. My town sets a lot of hopes on Christmas. The storekeepers do, anyway. What's it like at your home?"

Ann felt a small but savage stab of pain as she closed her eyes and visualized the Cay.

"Oh, they'll be having fun."

"And missing you like the dickens," said Jessie quietly. "That's what families are for: to love you and miss you and for you to love and to miss."

"I suppose so," Ann answered huskily.

"Nobody will be allowed to go home for Christmas, of course," said Jessie quietly, "unless she lives within a day's ride and can take one of her seven days' leaves."

Ann nodded. "Are you going home, Jessie?"

Jessie shook her head and managed a brave smile. "Oh, no," she said sturdily. "I'd rather save up my seven days and add it to my annual three weeks' vacation and have a whole month."

Ann smothered a faint sigh. "Oh, well, I guess we can live until next September and get that vacation all in a lump." She managed a grin that was not too convincing.

"Let's hope so." Jessie's smile was likewise brave. "And anyway, there's going to be a bash here at the hospital in the recreation room."

"A bash?" Ann repeated, puzzled.

"Oh, that's what some of the kids call it," she answered. "A dance and a big tree, with 'foolishment' gifts for everybody. And of course there will be the glee club from one of the colleges to sing carols, and special eats in the cafeteria. Everybody who isn't on duty is invited. And even the staff will look in for a few minutes to say 'Merry Christmas' and all that jazz."

"Sounds like fun," said Ann politely.

"Oh, it will be," Jessie answered. "What are you going to wear?"

"We're allowed to wear something other than our uniforms?"

"Oh, my stars and bars, pal, this is a festive affair—white tie and tails and stuff." Jessie laughed. "I can't decide whether to wear my gold lamé or the blue brocade, so I guess I'll just show up in my 'little nothing' navy blue. And 'little nothing' expresses it perfectly."

"Jessie, I'd love to lend you something," Ann began eagerly, and stopped at the sudden tautness on Jessie's gamine face.

"Thanks a couple of million—tax free, of course." Jessie tossed off her answer with an elaborately casual air. "But I like to travel under my own steam and under my own true colors. The 'little nothing' will be just fine."

"I didn't mean to offend you," Ann apologized awkwardly.

"Who's offended, you zany?" protested Jessie. "It's just that wearing lovely clothes like those you've got hanging in the closet could be habit-forming. But thanks a whole heck of a lot just the same. Why don't you wear that luscious cranberry-red chiffon? I'll bet you'll look like something Santy brought to some deserving young man for Christmas."

"Ha!" Ann mocked lightly. "That's a lovely thought."

"Ain't it just?" Jessie grinned. "What's your ward assignment this week?"

"The Children's Ward, and I'm the luckiest probie in the place," Ann answered in all sincerity.

"So you are, pal, so you are!" Jessie answered. "Well, we'd better run!"

"Not run, Jessie," Ann corrected her as they hurried down the corridor. "Remember, one of the first things they taught us is—hurry *fast* but don't run."

Jessie laughed and flung up a hand as she turned to the elevator that would take her to the mental ward on the top floor, where she was completing her four weeks' ward duty. And Ann went on swift feet to the wing that housed the Children's Ward.

As she entered it the ward-nurse looked up from her charts with frank relief.

"Am I ever glad to see you!" she confessed, and indicated the ward filled with obstreperous children. "There's word that Santa Claus will be here in an hour or two, and everybody is straining his eyes looking for him."

Ann looked over the large ward that held so many tiny beds, each occupied by a big-eyed, thin-faced child. In the center of the ward an enormous tree was receiving final decorative touches given by a group of twittering high school girls supervised by a couple of Gray Ladies who were checking lights and calling for a ladder so that the biggest star could be placed in the topmost branches.

Ann moved efficiently along the double row of beds, trying to soothe the patients' wild excitement.

She and Jessie had Christmas-shopped, and Ann's

presents for the Cay had long ago been lovingly and carefully packed and shipped. The village would be clamorous with excitement as laughing, chattering natives hurried about, caught up in the spell of the magic season. Any day was good for a fiesta if it gave an excuse to stop work; but this was the very best day of all. Tomorrow they would rest up and recover from the excitement of the day and be ready to return to work the day after.

Ann felt she could see the neat white cottages with their thatched roofs; giant poinsettias as large as dinner plates, ranging in color from the traditional deep red to a snowy white; hibiscus trying hard to out-bloom the poinsettias; tall palms, bent against the eternal wind from the ocean, their shadows moving darkly against the whiteness.

Up the hill in the hacienda, Clarita and Mary would be busy with the tree. She swallowed the lump in her throat and bent to take the temperature of a feverish small boy who wore a cast on his broken arm.

"Is Sandy Claws really-for-true coming here, Miss Nurse?" he asked softly, as though fearful that the question would bring a negative answer.

"Well, of course he is," Ann assured him, and entered the temperature on the chart, thankful that it was down a point since it had last been taken. "Can you imagine him not coming to see a good little boy like you?"

The boy's face was anxious.

"Well, I guess maybe I haven't been so awful good," he admitted. "You guess maybe he knows?"

"Well, now," said Ann thoughtfully, though there was a comforting twinkle in her eyes as she looked down at the small, worried face, "can you keep a secret?"

"Well, sure, Miss Nurse."

Ann leaned very low above him and whispered in the tone of a conspirator, "Then, I'll tell you a very fine secret. Santa Claus doesn't keep books on small boys and girls. Oh, he knows if you haven't been a good boy or girl, and he grieves about it. But when Christmas comes he just takes all the bad things you've done, rolls 'em up in a bundle and flings them into the furnace in his workshop before he starts out. He forgives you all your naughtiness; only you mustn't take advantage of him. Just because he forgives you doesn't mean you can go on being naughty. He expects you to be a better boy next year. Will you promise that?"

"Oh, yes, Miss Nurse," the small boy breathed, his thin face and tired eyes illumined by his eager smile. "I won' hit the baby any more."

"Well, you'd better not!" Ann warned him. "That's something Santa Claus finds very hard to forgive."

"I won't do it any more," the boy promised eagerly. "And when Mom calls me I'll answer right away. And I won't climb trees any more," he added as he cast a bitter eye on the cast that gripped his arm.

"Then you've got nothing to worry about," Ann assured him firmly. "Santa Claus has already forgiven you for being bad this year, and I'll bet you just about anything that he has a nice gift for you in his pack. But remember! Unless you're a good boy next year he may be so disappointed in you that he'll just forget to bring you a present."

"I'll 'member, Miss Nurse. I'll 'member real good!" the boy told her.

A little later there was a sound from the corridor outside the ward; a sound that brought instant silence: the unmistakable sound of sleigh bells!

Breathlessly still, the children listened, all eyes on the door; eyes touched with awe and wonder that lit up even the most pain-wracked small face. And then the door was flung open to reveal an enormously fat man with long white beard, his fire-engine-red suit belted about his ample waist with a wide black patent leather belt. Crowning his thick masses of snowy hair was a red velvet cap trimmed with white fur. And slung over his shoulder was an enormous and obviously well-filled pack!

For an instant the tableau held; and then the big man spoke in a great, booming voice.

"Mer-ry Christ-mas, children," he called out, and gave the traditional "Ho, ho, ho" that made his enormous stomach quiver engagingly.

Whoops of joy and mingled cries of "Merry Christmas, Sandy Claws," rang out through the ward. As Santa Claus came into the room and started down between the rows of beds, the children who were able to sat up; the others turned their pitiful faces and, wide-eyed as young sparrows at feeding time, watched him as he dived into his pack and came up with the first present.

Ann stood where she was as the man approached, pausing at each bed to make his presentation and to laugh and chortle happily with the children. When he reached the bed where she stood beside the boy with his arm in a cast, Santa's eyes twinkled warmly at her, and Ann smiled back at him.

"Well, well, well," chortled Santa Claus as he bent above the boy, "what have we here? Have you been a good boy?"

Color poured into the boy's thin face and his eyes fell away from the friendly, twinkling eyes bent down on him.

"Well, no, sir, Sandy Claws, I don't reckon I been very good," the boy admitted huskily. "I hit the baby; and I run and hide when Mommie calls me if I don't want to go in; and I fell out of a tree she told me not to climb and I busted my arm."

"Well, well," said Santa Claus, and there was a hint of censure in his voice beneath which the boy quailed slightly.

"Miss Nurse said if I promised to be *awful* good next year you'd forgive me and still bring me a present, though," the boy offered humbly.

Santa Claus straightened and his eyes met Ann's.

"So Miss Nurse says I'll forgive you if you promise to do better next year," Santa Claus mused aloud, balancing in his hand the gaily wrapped present meant for the small boy.

"Yes, sir, and I will, sir. I promise. I'll be *awful* good!" the boy pleaded. "Miss Nurse said you'd forgive me—"

"And we can't make a liar out of Miss Nurse, now can we?" asked Santa Claus, and put the package into the extended hand that closed eagerly over it. "Miss Nurse knew what she was talking about. But then, all the Miss Nurses here know what they're talking about, don't they? So you see you mind them, Buster. And I'll check on you next year, so you'd better be a good boy from now on. Promise?"

"Oh, yes, sir, I sure *do* promise!" stammered the boy, so excited that he scarcely knew what he was doing as he tried with his one hand to unwrap his package.

"Here, let me help you," said Ann gently, and unwrapped it.

It was a small toy truck, and the boy's eyes were beatific with happiness as he clutched it to his small bosom.

Santa Claus spoke softly to Ann, and in the hubbub his voice reached no further than her ears.

"Thanks for making Santa Claus a little more human, Ann," he murmured. Ann looked up at him, startled, as for a brief moment he eased the beard down and she saw David Lochran's laughing face before the masking beard snapped back into place. "I think Santy's entitled to a gift, don't you? How about saving me a dance tonight?"

"Why, of course, Santy," Ann murmured, her eyes bright with mockery, "if you're sure Mrs. Santy won't object."

David gave a resounding chortle and answered, "Oh, she's a very understanding woman."

He went on his way, completing the rounds, and Ann busied herself getting the children quieted down a little.

Chapter Four

The big recreation hall had been beautifully decorated, and there was an enormous tree in the day room. A four-piece orchestra composed of some of a neighboring college's music students was playing, and the floor had been carefully waxed.

When Jessie in the navy blue dress and Ann in her red chiffon entered, the room was already crowded and the laughter and the voices indicted the party was already well-started.

A young interne claimed Jessie for a dance, and Ann stood for a moment just inside the door, looking around her. People in the top echelon of the hospital as well as some of the training school staff were there, poised as if ready for instant flight.

David Lochran came swiftly into the room, glanced

about him and looked disappointed. Then he saw Ann and came toward her, his dark eyes sweeping over her in pleased surprise.

"Hi, this isn't really Miss Nurse, is it? Sure you're not a top-flight debutante strayed down here after hours?" he asked lightly.

"Most definitely not," Ann assured him. "Just a lowly probie out of uniform for a few hours."

David grinned at her and looked again about the room. "I don't see Julia around, do you?"

"She's on duty," Ann answered. "She has a patient who is post-operative and who demands special attention. She's very disappointed, but she promised to look in for a few minutes later on."

"She has no business letting them load her up with extra duty hours." David scowled. "I happen to know she's been on duty since eleven. She should have been free at seven."

"I know," Ann answered. "But almost everybody except the probies are doing extra duty. You did some yourself in the Children's Ward as Santa Claus. And a very fine job you did, too."

"Oh, that was fun." David dismissed it with an airy wave. "I was glad to escape from Emergency for a while. Rough down there during the holidays. I've never been able to understand why people choose holidays, especially holiday week-ends, to get themselves all smashed up in car wrecks, or get drunk and indulge in knife battles and the like. Have you?"

Ann laughed. "Oh, you forget, Doctor. I'm new here. Back home the only emergencies are snake bite, a gash with a machete or a triangle fight."

"And where would 'back home' be?" asked David.

"Spanish Cay," Ann answered, and swallowed the lump in her throat. "It's sort of a pin dot in the Caribbean, between Haiti and Honduras. It's not on a map, unless it's a very big map. But it's just about the most beautiful place in all the world."

Her voice sank to a husky whisper on the last words, and she blinked very hard against the threatening tears.

"Homesick, aren't you?" asked David gently.

She lifted swimming eyes to his, and her chin quivered as she fought against the tears.

"It's a sort of occupational hazard for probies, isn't it?" She managed an attempt at a damp smile.

"Why just for probies?" asked David gently. "It's universal, isn't it?"

"You, too?"

"No," answered David quietly. "You can't be homesick for something you've never had. I was left on a doorstep in the traditional manner."

Ann caught her breath and her eyes widened.

"You don't have a home?"

"Oh, I had foster parents," David told her. "They adopted me when I was three. They were very good to me, too, and saw to it I was educated and managed to hold onto life until I was fourteen. And then they were smashed up in a car crash on a Thanksgiving week-end. See now why I don't care too much for holiday week-ends?"

"I'm terribly sorry," Ann said gently.

David smiled at her.

"Thanks. It was a long time ago. I've adjusted to being a homeless somebody. The hospital is really my home, and it's been very good to me. Suppose you tell me about your home. The Cay sounds fascinating."

"Well, it's a small place and there are only a handful of white people there," Ann began. "There are two or three hundred native workers and their families. They look after the coffee crop, the banana plantation and the sugar cane. Clarita, my great-grandmother, is the *Señora* to whom they all look and whom they all love. And then there's Mary Delehenty, who lives with her and takes care of her; and Tad, Mary's son, who supervises the Cay's business operations; and the chief engineer, McGuire, an embittered Scot who doesn't like anybody or anything except his machinery and me—when I'm home."

Her chin quivered, and David said gently, "Well, go on. What's Christmas like down there?"

Ann described it to him: the midnight service in the church, which all the Cay's people would attend. And if, after the service was over, shadowy shapes crept through the white moonlight and out into the dense jungle to see old Mam' Cleo and have her brew them up a voodoo potion, that was something Clarita had never interfered with.

"Voodoo, eh?" David asked. "I understood that had been forbidden, at least in Haiti."

Ann gave him the ghost of a smile.

"I understand bootlegging and playing the numbers game have been forbidden in Capitol City," she mocked him lightly.

David laughed. "And so they have!" he agreed. "Tell me about Mam' Cleo. I've often heard of voodoo, and I think there are small, very carefully hidden 'pockets' of it in and around Capitol City, among the more illiterate."

So Ann told him about Mam' Cleo, the *mama-loi* or priestess of the forbidden cult which still operated in isolated regions of the swamp jungles.

David was listening to her as though completely fascinated when Julia Anderson, still in uniform, came swiftly toward them, her face anxious.

"Oh, David," she began, and then looked, startled, at Ann in her red frock. Ann stood up, smiling. "Why, Ann, I didn't recognize you! Don't you look beautiful!"

"Thank you, Miss Anderson," said Ann. "I know Dr. Lochran is glad you're here. I've been boring him to death bleating about my home and the weird things that go on there sometimes."

"I haven't been bored at all, Ann," David protested. And to Julia, "It sounds like an absolutely fascinating place. We were supposed to dance, but we seem to have forgotten all about that."

"It was my fault," Ann insisted.

Julia smiled at them both.

"He doesn't seem to have suffered," she answered. "But that's very good music. Should you waste it?"

She turned to David before Ann could manage an answer, and there was a troubled look in her eyes.

"I've got bad news, David," she told him. "That is, it's bad for me. I won't be able to go to the recital with you tomorrow night. I've got extra duty."

David scowled. "Oh, come now, Julie; you've been on extra duty for the last week. This is the second date you've broken."

"Well, don't think I like doing it, David," Julia told him. "And I'm not going to remind you of the ones we've had to break because *you* had extra duty. Remember the night you had to ride the bus? Ambulance duty certainly shouldn't be the responsibility of a resident."

David's grin was as rueful as hers.

"Sure, I know. But then I'm the rugged type. I can ride ambulance, serve extra hours in Emergency and in the wards, and it all adds up to training that will come in very handy. But for you I don't like it."

"Neither do I," Julia agreed. "But Lillian Esmond is ill with a virus, and Jody Johnson fell and broke her leg while she was helping to clean the o.r. after surgery. Clumsy of her, of course. Even a senior student nurse is supposed to be steadier on her feet than that. But that leaves two short on duty, and I have to fill in."

"Well, sure you do," David answered reluctantly. "But I'm very disappointed."

"Thanks, David." Julia smiled warmly at him. "I know the recital means a lot to you; you mustn't miss it. Blaine will be counting on you to be in the audience, since if it wasn't for you she would never have played piano again."

"She gives me too much credit," David answered. "I just made an extra-special effort to keep her cheered up and hopeful during her convalescence."

"And she was able to go back to her work, and now she's giving her recital for the home folks who have sponsored her training and then leaving for New York next week," Julia reminded him. "Unless you have to go on duty, David, you must go. She'd be heartbroken if you didn't."

She glanced at Ann. "Ann will be off duty tomorrow night. Why don't you take her?"

Ann said quickly, "Oh, but I'm sure Dr. Lochran must have someone else in mind."

And David's voice crossed hers, saying as quickly, "Oh, but Ann probably has plans of her own. It's Christmas Day."

"Have you, Ann?" asked Julia.

"Well, no, I haven't."

"It's a piano recital by a girl we all feel is brilliant and will some day be very famous," Julia told her. "You'll be proud some day to say 'Blaine Hanson? Oh, I heard her at her very first recital.' "

David laughed. "So now you see, Ann, you'd better go."

"If you're quite sure there isn't someone else you'd rather take."

David looked down at her for a moment, and Julia's eyes flashed from his intent face, the admiration in his eyes, to Ann's face that was flushed and eager and very lovely above the cranberry-red frock. The ghost of a shadow fled swiftly across her countenance but was gone before either Ann or David could see it.

"I'm quite sure," David said firmly.

"Good!" Julia beamed at them both. "Then it's all settled. I'll have to run now. Have fun, you two."

Ann watched her as she threaded her way through the laughing, chattering crowd and caught the gleam of her uniform as she vanished into the lobby.

"She's a lovely person, isn't she?" Ann said softly.

"One of the best!" David agreed. "Shall we use up some of this music? As Julia said, it's too good to lose."

Ann laughed as she slipped into his arms, and their steps matched as they moved smoothly out on the crowded floor.

David executed a very neat step and beamed happily as she followed the intricate movement expertly.

"The more I hear of Spanish Cay the more I like what I hear," he told her firmly.

"Then you must come and visit the Cay," said Ann happily. "You'd like it, I know. And Clarita would be so happy to have you."

"Who is Clarita?" asked David.

"My great-grandmother," answered Ann.

"And you call her Clarita?"

"It's what she wants to be called," Ann explained. "To the native workers and their families she's the *Señora.* But I've called her Clarita ever since I could toddle, and she loves it."

"One of these days," David told her as they executed the deft step once more and it flowed even more smoothly, "I have every intention of seeing the Cay and meeting Clarita and seeing the Caribbean."

"I'm going home for my three-week vacation at the end of my year," Ann told him. "It would be wonderful if you could go then."

She looked up at him eagerly. "Not but what you'd be more than welcome if you went any time at all. Clarita would love having you, and Tad and Dr. John would show you around and entertain you even if I wasn't there."

The dance ended, and for a moment they stood in the center of the dance floor. His arms dropped reluctantly from her waist as he studied her with a curious intentness that brought the warm color into her face.

"I'll wait until you're there," he told her.

"I'm glad," she answered, and added hastily, "I'd like to be there to be sure you don't miss any of the sights."

And then she laughed with a little gesture of deprecation.

"Not that there are so many sights to be seen," she apologized. "But I'd like to be sure you see them all. Aux Cayes is interesting; and there are some interesting spots that we can reach with the cabin cruiser we use for getting to and from and around."

"I'm intrigued," David assured her firmly. "I want especially to see the Cay with you, because it's obvious that you love it very much."

"I do, because it's home," said Ann, and there was the faintest possible quaver in her voice.

Chapter Five

The following day was a busy one, and Ann was late getting back to her room to dress for her date. Jessie had just come off duty and was lounging wearily on her bed when Ann came hurrying in.

Jessie sat up and stared at her.

"Hey, where are you rushing off to in such a swivet? Don't tell me they need you in o.r. to perform a craniotomy?" she demanded.

"And I hope they never do!" Ann said as she slid out of her uniform. "After that lecture we had in class about brain surgery, I hope sincerely I'll never even have to be a 'dirty nurse' at one. As for a scrub nurse—ugh!"

"Oh, well, I dunno," mused Jessie thoughtfully. "Darned interesting the way they use that electric knife to slice into a skull and prowl around inside somebody's brain!"

"Oh, *hush!*" pleaded Ann. "I think it's wonderful, too, but I want a lot more training and experience before I discuss the details."

Jessie grinned wickedly. "Wasn't it Oscar Wilde who said, 'Only the details are interesting'?"

"I wouldn't know," Ann admitted. "I wasn't permitted to read Oscar Wilde when I was growing up."

"Because of what, I wonder?" mused Jessie.

"Look," Ann changed the subject abruptly, turning from the closet to look anxiously at Jessie, "what does one wear to a piano recital on Christmas night?"

"Whoops!" Jessie sat bolt upright, her weariness temporarily forgotten. "Who's going to a piano recital on Christmas night?"

"Me," Ann told her with no regard for grammar. "Would the red dress I wore last night be all right? Or should it be something less formal?"

"Depends on whose recital and where it's held and who's taking you," Jessie answered curiously.

"I think Miss Anderson said somebody named Blaine Hanson, and Dr. Lochran is taking me. And I don't know where it's being held."

"You're going to the Hanson recital with Dr. Lochran? Saints preserve us forevermore!" Jessie gasped in astonishment. "How'd you manage that?"

"I didn't," Ann explained. "Miss Anderson was slated to go with him. She got extra duty because a couple of seniors had bad luck, and she told Dr. Lochran to take me. And he said if I wasn't doing anything, he'd be glad of my company. Now what will I wear?"

Jessie slid off the bed, her eyes round with awed admiration.

"Well, sir, I'd say no Big Sister was ever kinder to a kid sister," she commented. "The Hanson recital's being held in the auditorium of one of the churches, and I'm afraid the red dress from last night might be a wee bit too festive. I'd say this." She held up a turquoise wool dress, very smartly cut, with a bow of mink across the neckline. "Mink yet! Too bad you don't have a mink coat to wear with it."

"Now what," asked Ann as she made ready to change

into the turquoise wool, "would I be needing a mink coat for at Spanish Cay?"

"Not that I wish to be unkind, pal o mine," Jessie reminded her. "But you're nearly three years—two years and eight months, if you want to be stingy about it—from the Cay. And a mink coat would be mighty warm and snug the next three winters here in Capitol City. Maybe you'd better pick one up at the after-Christmas sales, huh? I'd be glad to go with you and help you choose."

Ann laughed. "Thanks, pal. But I have a hunch my cashmere coat will serve me faithfully for the next two winters and the third one I'll be back at the Cay!"

"True—too true!" Jessie agreed, reclining once more on her bed as Ann got into the turquoise wool. "I knew, the minute we looked at that dress at Rich's, that it was made for you, mink bow and all. You were sure you'd have very little opportunity to wear it! And now look!"

Ann finished zipping the dress, turned about before the small mirror above the dressing table and asked anxiously, "Does it look all right?"

"Like a million," Jessie assured her. "There's a big mirror in the day room. But you can safely take my word for it, honey: you look devastating, no less."

Ann rummaged in the closet, then looked over her shoulder at Jessie.

"Do I wear a hat?" she asked.

"Sure. It's in church," Jessie pointed out.

Ann brought out a small scrap of gold felt banded with gold satin, perched it on her head and looked anxiously at Jessie, who nodded approvingly.

"And I told you, when we found it in this Paris Hat Shop, that that hat was made for you," she said happily. "It does something for you, though I'm not quite sure what. Maybe I should change professions and become a fashion co-ordinator."

With the beige cashmere coat over her arm, Ann turned to Jessie and asked, "What are *you* going to do tonight?"

"Have turkey and trimmin's in the cafeteria with some of the other slaves. Then we're going to get together in somebody's room and tear the staff and the instructors and all the patients and R.N.s into little tiny pieces,'

Jessie said gaily. But there was the faintest possible quaver in her voice.

"Jessie darling, you're homesick," Ann accused her, her own voice not too steady.

"Well, aren't we all?" retorted Jessie.

Ann drew a deep, hard breath and managed a smile that was not too gay.

"I suppose so. But then we'd be just as homesick if we were tucked away in any other kind of school," she pointed out. "At least here we do know we are helping other people."

"Scat!" ordered Jessie with an unsteady laugh as she turned Ann about and pushed her toward the door. "I'm in no mood to listen to any lectures on the duties and responsibilities and rewards of a nursing career. Believe me, keed, I've heard 'em all, and I know most of them by heart. Oh, sure, I'm going to be a nurse and a darned good one; but leave us not indulge in any girlish chatter about high ideals and the like of that. Me, I'm homesick; and so are most of the other probies. You toddle on off with your elegant date and leave us to wallow in our misery!"

Impulsively, for she was not by nature demonstrative, Ann kissed Jessie's cheek and hurried out into the corridor and down to the "date parlor" on the first floor.

She looked swiftly about her as she hesitated in the doorway. The girls with whom she had lived the last four months were strangers to her now, as they had been last night, in their colorful frocks and their "non-regulation" hair-do's.

She couldn't find David in the brightly dressed, chattering group until suddenly a hand closed under her elbow and she looked up to see him beside her. He, too, looked strange in the well-cut business suit, his dark head bare.

"Let's get out of here before an emergency crops up." He urged her out of the building, and she gasped as the icy wind, stung with pellets of sleet, struck her full in the face.

"My car's right down here," David told her as he marched her half a block to where his car was waiting. "Here, pull that full collar up around your throat. Can't have you auditioning for pneumonia, you know."

He tucked her into the car, ran around to the other

side and slid behind the wheel. He glanced down at her as the motor purred reluctantly and said in a tone that was purely conversational, "By the way, did I remember to tell you that you look even lovelier than you did last night. And I hadn't imagined that was possible."

"Why, thank you, Doctor," she murmured sweetly, and laughed.

"Hey, skip the 'Yes, Doctor' for tonight, will you, Ann? Let's forget the hospital and all its rules and regulations just for once, shall we? You look beautiful; I feel festive; and we're going to hear some pretty wonderful music. So let's pretend I'm a young business executive out on a date with a glamorous young debutante."

Ann laughed joyously. "The young business executive I can accept; the glamorous debutante is beyond me."

"Swell! You accept the executive, I'll accept the debutante, and everything will be fine." He grinned at her. "You haven't had dinner, have you?"

"Come to think of it, I don't believe I have," Ann admitted, and added hastily, "But I'm not a bit hungry."

"Thanks for your loving care of my pocketbook," David told her gravely. "But I don't get out very often, and the bank-roll, even at a resident's monthly allowance, builds. So we'll have dinner and *then* we'll go to the recital. Turkey dinner?"

"Must we?"

"Eat? Well, of course we must. I've been in the operating room since noon, and I'm famished."

"I don't believe I'd be able to eat for a week after doing a stint in o.r.," Ann admitted impulsively.

David grinned at her understandingly.

"Still a bit squeamish? You aren't the girl who fainted at her first autopsy, are you?" he teased.

"No, that was Marian Gordon, and they sent her home," Ann said soberly, and barely repressed a shudder at the memory. "I didn't enjoy it, by several million light years. But the second wasn't nearly so bad; and now, while I still don't enjoy it, I can take it and remain on my feet."

"Good girl!" said David approvingly, and added, "I imagine you're as fed up with turkey as I am; what would you like?"

"You really want to know?"

"I wouldn't have asked you otherwise. Name it and

you can have it, if the town provides it. And they provide just about everything from hummingbird's wings on toast to rattlesnake meat."

"I'd like a hamburger," Ann told him firmly, "or a hot dog."

David stared at her with raised eyebrows.

"You mean that?"

"I wouldn't have said it otherwise," she mocked him gaily.

"Then a hamburger it is, and I fancy the thought myself," David told her. "You really *are* the perfect date for a young medico who's fighting to win his spurs."

"Oh, no, remember? I'm a glamorous debutante dating a young business executive. And hamburgers for dinner are 'seeing how the other half lives.' "

David laughed. "Gastronomical slumming, eh?" he teased her as he parked the car beside a small white building bathed in the fierce glow of neon lights.

They ran across the parking lot. David swung open the door, and a blast of warmth, redolent with onions and frying hamburgers, hit them in the face. Perched on stools in front of the white-tiled counter, they ate enormous buns and succulent and juicy hamburgers with slices of raw onions on top.

Ann gravely inspected the onion and looked at David like a wary child.

"Do we dare?" she asked hesitantly.

David took an enormous bite of his sandwich, biting through the onion, and grinned at her.

"It's illegal or at least subversive to eat hamburgers without onion," he told her gravely. And as though each thought that very funny, they laughed joyously.

"One thing sure," Ann told him, consuming her own sandwich, onion and all, "no matter how big the crowd is we'll be sure to have plenty of room. We'll smell so of onions that nobody will want to sit near us!"

"Now that's a thought." David grinned. "Maybe we should have ordered garlic!"

"Oh, please!" Ann protested, laughing. "Will there be a tremendous crowd at the recital?"

"I doubt it," David told her. "After all, it *is* Christmas night, and in Capitol City that's a night when a lot of people want to be at home. But Blaine is very much admired, and the civic club that has sponsored her training and will continue to sponsor it is trying to get as big a turn-out as possible. But on a stormy night like this, when most people with homes like to be in them, I am afraid there won't be too big a crowd. It is a sort of farewell to Blaine before she goes away to continue her training. She's going to be a really fine concert artist or die in the attempt."

"She sounds like a wonderful person," said Ann soberly.

"She's all of that," David answered. "About fourteen months ago, she injured her left hand and was in the hospital for treatment. She was despondent, sure she'd never play again. But the hospital pulled her through. It's a great place for miracles, is Blaylock Memorial."

"From what Miss Anderson said, I think you must have played a large part in bringing that miracle to pass," Ann told him.

David made a little deprecating gesture.

"Oh, I did what I could because I admired her so much," he answered carelessly. "I read everything I could find about such injuries and worked to cure her depression, which I was convinced was the most serious part of her injury. She rallied, and now she's giving a recital. If we want to be in our seats when it begins, it behooves us to get moving."

They came out of the hamburger house and moved through sleet and snow to where his car was parked. Carefully, slowly, he managed the drive to the church across town. When they came into the amber-lighted church and he saw that many of the pews were already filled, he grinned down at Ann.

"Quite a crowd,'" he beamed as they seated themselves. "And we're just in time."

The auditorium lights went down and a spotlight touched the stage, highlighting the grand piano in the center. From the side entrance at the left a woman moved into the spotlight. She was tall, angular, her long black dress with its high round neckline sweeping about her feet. Her hair was sandy-yellow and roughly cut, so that her head was like a large, shaggy chrysanthemum topping her tall, thin body.

She seated herself at the piano, seeming scarcely conscious of the audience that watched her. For a moment her long, thin white hands were poised above the keyboard and then she brought them down in a crashing crescendo and began the first number; a difficult, brilliant number that brought rounds of applause when she had finished. She sat at the keyboard, waiting until the applause had died to silence, neither acknowledging it nor smiling. She seemed merely to be waiting impatiently for the noise to die away so she could proceed with the program.

She played brilliantly, and her numbers were carefully selected to show off her skill and her virtuosity. At the conclusion of the first half of the program she stood up and accepted the applause without a smile, merely bowing her chrysanthemum-head in acknowledgement. And then she sat down once more, and the rippling strains of a well-loved Christmas carol flowed from beneath her fingers. She played a group of carols and then ended with the most beloved of all, "Silent Night."

As the lovely melody crept out over the hushed audience, Ann caught her breath in a small, silent gasp. Probably at this very moment down at the Cay, Clarita, Dr. John, Tad, Mary and the chief engineer, having finished a marvelous dinner, were listening to this same melody.

"Crying?" David whispered to her, and his hand enfolded hers.

"They're playing this very carol at the Cay right this minute." She could not keep back the words. "It's Clarita's favorite."

David's hand held hers warmly, and there was comfort in the touch.

When the last lovely note had died away, Blaine sat for a long moment, her hands clasped in her lap, her head bowed, her eyes closed. And then she lifted her head, rose to her feet and stood leaning against the curve of the piano as though she needed its support as the audience crowded forward to congratulate her and wish her success.

David and Ann moved forward with the others, and as they approached Blaine she glanced at them. She moved forward and held out both hands.

"Dr. Lochran! How very kind of you to be here!" Her voice was rough, faintly husky, as though she did not use it a great deal.

"You didn't think I'd miss it, did you?" David's two hands clasped hers and held them tightly as he beamed at her. "I'm so very proud of you, Blaine. You were magnificent."

"Thanks; you're very kind," said Blaine, and glanced at Ann with a faint frown. "Julia's not with you?"

"Extra duty," David answered, and presented Ann.

Blaine said curtly, "How do you do?" and then in a tone of surprise, "You've been crying! Why?"

"How could I help it? The music was so beautiful," Ann told her honestly. "I've never heard 'Silent Night' played so gloriously. And the others numbers were grand, too, the Rachmaninoff *Prelude* especially."

Blaine made a disdainful gesture. "The first half of the program was fireworks," she mocked, "to prove what I could do. But the carols were from the heart, not the hands or the brain."

"I felt that," Ann said quietly. "That's why I cried."

For a moment Blaine's gray eyes widened with surprise, and then she turned her head and smiled at David.

"What a very nice child, Dr. Lochran. Thank you for bringing her," she said lightly.

"No, Miss Hanson, I'm the one to thank him for that," Ann said in an impulsive rush of words. "It's been a glorious experience hearing you; all my life I'm going to boast about it."

Miss Hanson looked at her with a warm pleasure that transformed her angular, plain face into something faintly approaching beauty. But all she said was a simple heartfelt "Thank you!"

The press of others who wished to congratulate the pianist pushed them on. Back in the parking lot, David looked down at Ann and smiled.

"And now to get back inside the walls of the nurses' dorm before they lock the doors on you," he said lightly, deliberately bringing an end to the tension that she had felt from the moment the first exquisite notes of "Silent Night" had swept through the auditorium.

Back at the hospital, she stood on the steps of the dormitory and tried to thank him for the wonderful evening. But he said gaily, "I should be, and I am, thanking you for making it a memorable evening indeed. I hope our off-duty hours may match up again sometime! Good night."

Ann went into the dormitory where a sleepy senior student, a member of the student council, guarded the sign-in book. As she wrote her name opposite the hour of her return, the nurse yawned and then smiled at her.

"Hooray for you, probie. You made it with fifteen minutes to spare," she said. "Be thankful you're a probie, not an R.N. It's a rough night in the old place this night."

"Well, Merry Christmas anyway," Ann offered as she hurried to the elevator and up to her own room where Jessie was sleeping soundly.

Chapter Six

As the days and weeks slid by and winter gave way to early spring, Ann and the others in her class concentrated on preparing for the examination that would, as Jessie expressed it, separate the probies from the first year student nurses. The training was intensified. There were fifteen to twenty-four hours' work a week in class and laboratory; two to ten hours a week in the wards. And there were long study periods.

As the months passed Ann could tell when spring had come just by the flowers that came in daily for the patients. But there was a lovelier and more exciting way of watching the coming of spring.

Across the street from the vast buildings that housed Blalock Memorial there was a small triangle of park. Bordered on three sides by paved streets along which traffic flowed in a noisy and apparently never-ending stream, it was an oasis of velvety green grass, in the center a large fountain that was illuminated by colored lights at night. And bordering the walks and splashing the slopes of the park were thousands of tulips. Each year several thousand more were planted, and each spring the city held a Tulip Festival in the park. A queen was elected, and her court, and there were Dutch costumes and wooden shoes and dances, and it was all a highlight of spring, not only for the city itself but for the personnel and patients of the hospital.

So as the grass greened in the park, and the tulips lifted their green spikes, and the dogwood trees flung out branches of starch-white, the park was a favorite spot for such nurses and probies as had an hour off duty. Jessie and Ann often bought sandwiches at the hamburger stand on the corner and went down into the park during lunch hour. Their pink uniforms and white aprons against the green grass made a pretty picture. Many office workers from nearby skyscrapers also had their lunch hours there, and Ann and Jessie relaxed and chatted of their plans for the future.

The written examinations would take place in May. And as the time approached both girls admitted to a bad case of jitters.

"If I flunk this examination and am given the bounce from here, Ann, I won't dare show my face at home," Jessie said one evening as they were getting ready for bed. "It's different for you. Nobody's going to throw it in your teeth that they sponsored you, and you can go home with a free conscience."

"And that's where you're very wrong, Jessie," Ann answered. "I can't let Clarita down; most of all, I can't fail our people who need me. For their sake, I don't *dare* wash out! You won't either. We've worked hard and we've studied hard—"

"Uh-huh," Jessie assured her grimly. "And I bet the minute I get in that examination room with the papers all spread out before me and look at the questions, I'll draw a perfect blank. I'll be so scared I'll forget everything I've learned."

"You will if you keep thinking so," Ann pointed out. "Remember that! If you *think* you're going to fail, you will. That's negative thinking, Jessie. And it's something you and I can't afford."

Jessie nodded soberly. "You're a comfort, pal. You're going to make a fine nurse, if we ever get through the next two years."

"We will," Ann assured her. "We've *got* to!"

A few days before the examination was scheduled, Ann came back from duty to their room and found Jessie face down on her bed, weeping as though her heart would break. At Ann's swift, anxious query, Jessie merely buried her face a little more deeply against her pillow and held out a scrap of paper.

With her heart in her throat for fear of what she would

read in the paper extended to her, Ann took it. Written in the scrawl of a third or fourth grader was a note that read:

"Dear Jess: Mom don't want you to know it, but us kids think you oughter come home for a little while anyway. Pop got hurt real bad at the sawmill, and he'd sure love to see you. Couldn't you come and see him for a little while? Yours truly, Johnny. PS: Don't let Mom know I wrote, will you?"

"You must go, Jessie," said Ann swiftly.

Jessie's head rolled in a negative shake on the pillow.

"They won't let me," she wailed, her voice caught with sobs. "I asked Miss Anderson. She said that if I went I'd have to resign from the class. She says students, especially probies, aren't expected to leave the school because of family crises or for any other reason. And Pop—oh, Ann, maybe I could do something for him. If I could just see him and talk to him and hug his neck like I did when I was a little kid—Oh, Ann, he's so good! And he's worked so hard for all of us, and now I can't even go to see him when he's hurt!"

She buried her face in the pillow, and her whole body shook with the intensity of her sobbing.

Ann looked down at her for a moment. Then, without giving herself a chance for a second thought, she hurried out of the room and down the stairs and across to the superintendent's office. Dr. John had said that she might talk to Miss Marshall if something drastic came up; and this surely was.

The nurse-secretary on duty in Miss Marshall's office looked up from her typewriter, and a frown touched her face as she saw the uniform that marked Ann as a probationer.

"Yes?" she asked.

"May I—I'd like—that is, would Miss Marshall see me for just a moment?" stammered Ann.

"Of course not," said the other crossly, "you have your own faculty advisers, your Big Sister. You're not supposed to come to Miss Marshall unless she sends for you. And if she does, watch it!"

Her eyebrows went up slightly, and she asked sharply, "Did she?"

"No," Ann answered. "Dr. John said that if I needed to see her very badly, I'd find her available. Well, I *do* need to see her, and it's very urgent. It's just about a matter of life and death."

The secretary was just about to refuse again when the door of Miss Marshall's private office opened and she came out with a chart in her hand.

"Lucy, attend to this, please," she began. Then she saw Ann, and her large, plain face altered. "What are you doing here?"

"Please, Miss Marshall, I must speak to you. It's terribly important—"

"Who are you?" demanded Miss Marshall sternly.

"I'm Ann Galt, from Spanish Cay, and Dr. John sponsored me here," Ann answered.

Miss Marshall's carefully controlled features just barely missed registering surprise, and then she said curtly, "Well, come in."

She turned and strode back into her office; a tall, heavily built woman whose white uniform was so crisp with starch that it crackled when she seated herself behind the desk.

"So Dr. John sent you to us," she mused. "Well, what is this terribly urgent matter that makes you go over the heads of your own superiors and come to me?"

"It's this," said Ann huskily, and laid the note before her.

Miss Marshall picked it up and frowned as she read it. Then she handed it back to Ann and said crisply, "I'm sorry, but she may not go."

Ann stared at her incredulously. "But, Miss Marshall, it's her own father. He's badly hurt. He may die!"

Miss Marshall nodded, and though she seemed completely undisturbed there was a look in her tired eyes that was not without compassion.

"I'm very sorry, Galt, but the rules of the training school are inflexible. No student may leave the class for family reasons or any other reason unless she resigns. She can't be re-instated."

"Miss Marshall, I'll do Jessie's work for her while she's gone."

"It's not the work that's important, Galt," said Miss Marshall. "The hospital could manage without her quite easily; the point is that she can't manage without the hospital, if she expects to complete her training. If she missed as much as one day of training, she'd never be able to catch up with the class again. I'm very sorry, Galt, but it's out of the question. If she wishes to resign from the class—"

"She doesn't, Miss Marshall. She loves it and she wants very much to finish."

"Then she must not go home," said Miss Marshall firmly.

Ann cried out, unable to check the words, "But, Miss Marshall, that's inhuman! Her own father! And you insist she turn her back on him. What kind of a nurse would she be if she could do that?"

"A very good one," said Miss Marshall coolly. "If she can put her duty, her responsibilities while she is training, ahead of her family needs and any such calls as this, then she will be a nurse who will accept both discipline and responsibility. And that's the kind of nurse Blalock Memorial wants to turn out."

"I still think it's inhuman," Ann cried out recklessly.

Miss Marshall rose from her chair, and to Ann there was something terrifying in her rock-hard face, her cold eyes.

"Be very careful, Galt," she said quietly. "You are being impertinent and rude. I will not tolerate such behavior on the part of an R.N. and certainly not from a probationer. Discipline is one of the most important things in a place of this sort; I would not like to have to send you back to the Cay and Dr. John for insubordination. Run along now."

Ann hesitated for just a moment, but the cold, hard look of the woman finally made her turn, her shoulders sagging, and go back out into the corridor. She went back to her room and to Jessie with her mouth a tight line of anger.

Jessie rolled over on the bed and looked up at her. "Who'd you see, Ann?' she asked fearfully.

"Miss Marshall."

Jessie gasped.

"And I could have saved myself the bother," Ann told her grimly.

"Well, that's what Miss Anderson said." Jessie hiccoughed, rubbed her face childishly, and then the tears came anew. "Oh, Ann, my Pop is just about the grandest man you ever saw. He's so proud of me, and if he wants to see me and he's badly hurt—" Once more she buried her face in the tear-sodden pillow.

Ann sat beside her, made soothing noises, patted her heaving shoulder and felt sick with pity.

"If you resigned from the class, Jessie—" she began tentatively.

Jessie shook her head.

"I couldn't, Ann, after all the people at home, the women at the church, just about everybody worked so hard to get me entered here as a student. They're counting on me to come back and be county nurse for a miminum of one year after I get my pin. And Pop just about expired with pride at the party they gave to send me off up here. It would just about break his heart if I came home with my tail tucked between my legs! It would be bad enough and shameful enough if I 'washed out.' But if I just gave up and came home because he was hurt—why, he'd always feel he'd ruined my life, and he wouldn't be able to take that! He grieves because he's been unable to do much for his kids. There are so many of us. I'm the oldest and if I get to be a nurse then I can take some of the burden off his shoulders and see the other kids get an education. And that's terribly important to Mom and Pop. They look at us and at each other and say, 'Our kids are going to have a better chance than we did!' "

There was a light tap at the door, but neither of the two girls heard it. The door swung open and Julia Anderson stood there for a moment before either of them was aware of her presence. Then they scrambled to their feet and stood at attention.

"Relax, kids," said Julia with a friendly smile. "This is just a friendly call from Big Sister."

"Won't you come in and have the chair?" Ann suggested with frosty courtesy as she indicated the tiny room's one chair.

"Thanks," said Julia, and for a moment her eyes took Ann in from head to foot. "I understand you went to

Miss Marshall to ask permission for Jessie to go home for a visit, Ann."

"The grapevine works almost as well here as on the Cay, apparently," Ann answered.

Julia made a gesture of annoyance.

"Now see here, Ann. There's no point in behaving like a spoiled child who is told it must obey rules and regulations set up for its own protection." Julia's tone had a faint but perceptible edge. "I'm terribly sorry that Jessie can't be excused from classes to go home; but under the circumstances, since both of you studied the rules before you were accepted as probationers, I see no reason you should feel, as you apparently do, that the hospital is being cruel in demanding that you obey them."

Ann locked her teeth against a retort that she knew would be unwise. Julia waited for Ann to answer; and when she didn't Julia put her arm about Jessie's shoulders and drew her down on the edge of the tumbled bed.

"I know it seems cruel, Jessie dear, but you must realize that, especially at this stage of your training, being away from classes for even twenty-four hours is out of the question," she said in a tone completely different from the one she had used to Ann. "Now, with examinations coming up, and with your class-room hours and laboratory and ward duty, can't you see how much essential training you would lose if you went home?"

"I suppose so," Jessie answered huskily.

"Of course you do. You want to be a registered nurse, don't you?" Julia asked gently.

"More than anything in the world," Jessie answered, and her breath caught on a sob. "But I also want to see my father who's badly hurt."

"Do you want to go home badly enough to give up your training?"

"Oh, no, I couldn't do that!"

Julia said very quietly, "Jessie, in the years ahead when you are an R.N. and taking care of a dangerously ill patient, there may be family needs that you will have to face; you will have to choose between abandoning the patient whom your Nightingale Oath assured you was your first duty and letting someone else attend to the family needs. If you don't feel you can measure up to a decision like that, and make the right one as a dedicated nurse, then it would be better for you to resign from the class and go home now."

Jessie drew a long, unsteady breath and managed a grimace that tried unsuccessfully to be a smile.

"I'm staying," she said.

"Good girl!" Her words were simple, but the tone made them an award of merit. "Have your folks a telephone?"

"Oh, yes! But it would cost a lot to phone them."

"Be my guest." Julia smiled at her. "Come on down to the lobby and shut yourself up in a booth and telephone your mother. Find out just how your father is. Your brother's note was written when?"

"Night before last," Jessie answered, "while he was doing his homework, and mailed on his way to school yesterday morning. I don't know how he got a stamp without somebody finding out. He could pay for one, of course, but how he could get to the post office, which is clear across town from school, to buy a stamp I don't know."

"Well, you've already learned here that twenty-four hours make a big difference in a patient's condition," Julia comforted her, and added swiftly as she saw the gleam of fear in Jessie's eyes, "And most of the time it's a change for the better."

Jessie stood up, and Julia said gently, "It's going to be for the better, Jessie. You just hang onto that thought."

Jessie said radiantly, "Oh, I will, I will. And thank you for letting me telephone them."

"Any time at all, Jessie," Julia told her, and glanced at Ann. "Coming, Ann?"

"Of course," said Ann stiffly, and followed them out of the room.

Downstairs in the big lobby, there was a row of telephone booths. Ann stopped at the desk, got some change and came back to one of the booths. She stacked quarters and dimes on the shelf, motioned to Jessie and said, 'Hop to it, Jessie!"

Radiant, despite her tear-stained face, Jessie stepped inside the booth and drew the door shut.

Ann sat on a bench across from the rack of booths and watched Jessie's face through the glass door. She watched, too, the anxious, worried people who came and went; the nurses going off duty; the internes who hurried in or out.

"A little world all its own with its own rules and regulations that have to be like the laws of the Medes and the Persians," Julia said quietly as she dropped down on the bench beside Ann.

Ann tilted her chin a trifle, and her voice was cool as she answered, "A sort of despotic dictatorship, isn't it?"

"It isn't at all, Ann." Julia's tone was curt. "But if you feel so deeply that it is, then I'd suggest that perhaps you made a mistake in deciding to be a nurse."

"I didn't decide," Ann answered grimly. "There are a lot of things I'd rather be. My coming here was Clarita's idea, not mine. There has to be someone trained in medicine on the Cay because of the people who work for us. Dr. John is reaching the end of his ability to take care of them; and there is no man in our family since my brother was killed. He was almost finished with his training, and would have been licensed and free to return as medical officer for the Cay in less than a year."

"I'm sorry," said Julia. "I didn't know."

"How could you?" Ann shrugged wearily. "It's not something I go around bleating about. I'm going to be a nurse if it kills me."

Her voice shook faintly, and Julia's hand touched hers.

"It won't, Ann, believe me, although there may be times like these when you almost wish it would," she answered. "I know, because I've been through it all myself. They always tell you the first year of nurse's training is the hardest. But don't you believe them, Ann! The third one is just as rugged."

Ann hesitated and then said awkwardly, "I'm sorry I made a fuss and went to Miss Marshall."

"So long as you don't do it again," Julia forgave her. "Hereafter, when something comes up that neither you nor I can handle, see the superintendent of the nurses' school. Don't go to Miss Marshall. That's like a buck private in the Army who's dissatisfied with something and goes straight to the commanding officer, instead of through channels: his corporal, then his sergeant, then the lieutenant and so on."

"And if he lives long enough he finally reaches the general?" asked Ann.

"If his problem is of sufficient importance," Julia agreed. "Forgive me if this is something I shouldn't ask; but if you were in Jessie's spot, and it was your great-grandmother who needed you, what would you have done?"

Ann set her teeth hard.

"I'd have tried to remember that I'm here because she wanted me to be and that I'm learning something that will eventually benefit the entire Cay, and I'd have stayed," she answered. "But that doesn't mean I wouldn't have hated the regulations and rules that said I had to."

Julia nodded as though that made perfect sense.

"Well, of course you would," she said pleasantly. "After all, nobody enjoys obeying rules all the time. But we have to, or the whole world would be in chaos."

The door of the telephone booth swung open and Jessie came running across the lobby. One glimpse of her joyous face told them that the news was good. As she reached them she flung herself into Julia's arms and clung tightly.

"Oh, Pop is better!" She glowed. "They don't need me at all. He's badly hurt, but Dr. Fleming says he'll be all right in a few weeks. And Mom was so glad to hear my voice we both cried. And she brought Johnny to the phone, and he cried, too. I think that was because he was afraid he might get punished for writing to me. But Mom promised he wouldn't be."

She paused for breath, and when Ann and Julia had expressed their delight at the news, she went on to Julia, "I can't ever thank you for suggesting I call them."

"Sure you can!" Julia smiled at her. "All you've got to do is pass next week's examination with flying colors so I can boast about my kid sister. And don't think I won't, either!"

Jessie drew a deep breath of joy and relief.

"Oh, it was wonderful just to hear their voices and to have Mom give me some of the news," she breathed. "I'm afraid we were very extravagant with your money, Miss Anderson, but I'll pay you back."

"You do and I'll smack you," Julia said firmly as they turned toward the elevators. "This calls for a celebration. You two run up and get into 'civvies,' and we'll go out to dinner and a gay, exciting movie that has a lot of laughs in it. Scamper now, both of you!"

She pushed them into the elevator and smiled as she stepped back.

Jessie said as the elevator rose, "Oh, isn't she wonderful?"

Julia was waiting for them when they came down to the lobby. She was slender and smart in a tailored suit and a scrap of a hat, with soft furs about her shoulders.

The man talking to Julia turned as Jessie and Ann hurried up, and David Lochran smiled at them.

"Hi, there," he greeted them. "Dinner and the movies, eh?. Aren't you the elegant ladies of leisure?"

"We've earned a few hours off, Doctor," Julia told him demurely. "Haven't we, kids?"

"I'm not sure about us, but I know you have, and it's pretty swell of you to spend your free time with us!" Jessie said eagerly. "But if Dr. Lochran is free and you've got a date with him, we could go alone."

"Now that's what I call a sweet and considerate gal." David grinned at her warmly. "But I've got to be 'on call' in case of an emergency. I don't get a night off for three weeks."

Julia smiled at him, tucked a hand through Jessie's arm and reached her other hand tentatively toward Ann, who flushed but yielded her arm graciously.

"You must get Ann to tell you about that absolutely fabulous Cay that is her home," David told Julia as his eyes focused on Ann. "She's invited me to visit it when I'm through the salt mines here and she gets her vacation. I'm planning to take her up on that invitation. Maybe if you are *very* nice to her, Julia, she might include you in the invitation, since we are both getting through here at about the same time."

"Oh, but Miss Anderson *is* included in the invitation," Ann said quickly. "I'll get Clarita to write both of you, and we can all go down together."

"Wonderful!" said Julia smoothly. "And now shall we get going?"

David held out a key-ring. "Use my car; it's in the parking lot."

"Greater friendship hath no man than that he should lend his cherished car to a woman driver!" Julia mocked him.

"You get one single tiny scratch on it and I'll report you to the chief of staff!" David warned her.

"A fate worse than death!" Julia breathed in make-believe awe.

David laughed, and as the three went across the lobby and out into the cool spring night, Ann looked back over her shoulder and saw him still standing there watching them. He put up his hand and wiggled his fingers in a gay, boyish little salute, and then the three girls stepped out of the lobby and down the steps to the parking lot.

"He's nice, isn't he?" Jessie asked happily.

"Very," said Julia briefly. And as she fitted the key into the lock of the car door, she glanced just once at Ann with an oddly taut expression on her lovely, well-controlled face.

Chapter Seven

The whole training class was in a twitter as examination day dawned. They filed into the big room where they had worked at their books and listened to lectures from various members of the nursing school and the staff. The desks were cleared of everything except the examination papers.

They waited tensely, and when the teacher read out the first question there was a little breath of relief that was like a small wind running through a dry corn-field. The teacher laughed.

"Well, have fun with that one," she warned them. "They get harder as we go along, I promise you."

But as the hours went on and the examination progressed, most of the girls found their memories and their training paying off; and at the end of the day as, completely exhausted, they trailed away to their rooms, most of them were at least mildly optimistic that they had made a passing grade. And when, after what seemed to them an eternity of delay, the grades were posted on the bulletin board in the day room, there were squeals of delight, breathless cries of, "I made it! I made it! Oh, I don't see how I did." Inevitably there were also a few who looked at the list, turned, white-faced and their eyes glazed with tears, and vanished to their own quarters to pack and return home.

Jessie and Ann were in the top five bracket. They stood looking at their names, and then Jessie said softly, her tone touched with awe, "We made it, Ann! We really made it! What about that!"

"Well, didn't you expect to?" Ann teased her.

"Expect to? Zounds, no! I only hoped!" Jessie drew a deep hard breath. "Now if we can just make the next two years and three months!"

"Well, let's hope we make that, too," suggested Ann.

"Oh, I'm hoping like crazy!" Jessie answered. "I'm going to do more than hope. I'm going to work myself silly!"

"I have a hunch we'll both have to," Ann reminded her. "I hear the going gets really tough from here on."

Jessie eyed her severely. "Of course up to now it's been just a breeze."

"Ask one of the senior students and see what she tells you," Ann warned her.

"I did," Jessie admitted. "I asked our beloved Big Sister, and she said just that. But she seems to think we can have a good chance if we work like the dickens, eat our spinach, rise promptly when one of our superiors enters a room, keep our mouths shut and act like good little girls."

"Sounds entrancing, doesn't it?" Ann asked ruefully.

Jessie chuckled. "Oh, well, from now on we can snoot the new probies, even while we're being very respectful to our superiors, and who knows? Three months from now we can go home to see our folks!"

There was considerable excitement as the girls of the new first year student class were fitted for their uniforms. Gone were the pink chambrays and the enveloping white aprons and the bare heads; after the candle-lighting ceremony the following night, they would have small white caps to wear. And after the completion of each year of their training they would add a small blue band to the caps; until that longed-for day when they emerged as full-fledged R.N.'s, with a cap and a pin to tell the whole world who and what they were. Their new uniforms were blue chambray, and their aprons boasted bibs, and they twittered like a nestful of birds as they prepared for the ceremony to be held in the auditorium.

The huge room was well-filled half an hour before the ceremony was to begin. The music began and they started forward, moving slowly in step to the music, their proud young heads held high, their eyes on the spot at the end of the aisle where the chaplain stood waiting for them. His plump, ruddy face beneath his thin fringe of white hair was warm and friendly. The eyes that had looked on much misery and suffering and sinning were compassionate and gentle.

As the double row of girls reached him and spread in a semicircle before him, he recited the invocation and added a few words of his own that told them how proud he was of his office that could thus welcome them into a noble and rewarding profession.

Each girl held a tall, unlighted candle.

When the invocation was finished, the girls all lifted their heads and, still holding their unlighted candles, recited the pledge that is a tradition in their profession, the Florence Nightingale pledge.

> "I solemnly pledge myself before God and in the presence of this assembly:
> To pass my life in purity and to practice my profession faithfully.
> I will abstain from whatever is deleterious and mischievous, and will not take or knowingly administer any harmful drug. I will do all in my power to maintain and elevate the standards of my profession, and will hold in confidence all personal matters committed to my keeping, and all family affairs coming to my knowledge with the practice of my profession.
> With loyalty will I endeavor to aid the Physician in his work and devote myself to the welfare of those committed to my care."

The words were spoken solemnly; at the finish, each girl lifted her head proudly, and it was clear that the words had found an abiding place in their young hearts.

And then a group of Big Sisters came down the opposite aisle, each carrying a lighted candle. And as the Big Sisters reached the front of the auditorium, each stopped in front of the two girls who had been her charges for the past nine months; and each lighted candle was tipped to light the wicks of the candles held by her charges.

Ann blinked back tears and managed a faintly tremulous smile as Julia brought her candle into flame, and Julia said softly, "Well done, little sister. I'm very proud of you."

Before Ann could manage an answer, Julia had lit the flame of Jessie's candle and had spoken the same words, and Ann felt a trifle deflated. Obviously, she told herself, the words were routine at such a moment and therefore all but meaningless.

There was a brief silence as the lighted candles of the Big Sisters were placed on the small table; and then each came forward carrying the small white caps that were the sign and symbol that each girl had been accepted as a first year student in the training school.

And then it was Vada Marshall's duty to make a brief speech welcoming the girls into the school's first year training class. They were no longer probationers; they were student nurses! As Vada spoke, in a calm, assured voice, her eyes traveled from one bright, alert young face to another until they met Ann's cool, frosty regard and lingered for a barely perceptible instant. But the expression in Vada's eyes did not change, nor did her voice falter as she went on.

And then it was over. The candles were blown out and placed on the table beside those the Big Sisters had set there. The ranks broke, and there were gay squeals of joy as each girl turned to greet members of her family and admiring friends.

Jessie smiled ruefully at Ann.

"Oh, well," she said hardily, "I didn't expect any of my folks to be here, and I don't suppose you did either."

At that moment a woman spoke behind Jessie, and Jessie whirled, startled, incredulous, to look at a tall, angular work-worn woman in a shabby spring coat and a hat so out of style that it was almost back in again. Happy tears slid down the tired face, and the unpainted mouth wore a termulous smile.

"Mom!" Jessie cried shakily as the two met and fell into each other's arms. "Oh, Mom, I didn't know you were coming."

"You surely didn't think I'd miss seeing you capped and pledged, honey, even if I had to walk every step of the three hundred miles!" The woman laughed through her tears, holding Jessie close to her. "Mrs. Hawkins and Mrs. Culver decided it would be a shame if somebody of your family wasn't here, so we drove up. Honey, we're all so proud of you. Pop's just fine; and he says to hurry up and get through your training and come on home, because he misses you!"

Ann tried to slip away, but Jessie stopped her.

"Come here and meet my Mom, Ann!" she cried, her voice tremulous with happy surprise. "Oh, Mom darling, it's so good to see you. This is my friend, Ann Galt."

Mrs. Allen turned to Ann as the other women surrounded Jessie. And the smile on Mrs. Allen's care-worn face made it very nearly beautiful as she put out her ungloved hands that made no apologies for their work stains.

"I'm real proud to meet you at last, Ann," she said warmly. "Jessie has written us a lot about you, and we're all so grateful for what you've done for her."

"Oh, my goodness, Mrs. Allen, you have no call to be grateful to me," Ann protested. "She's done a lot more for me than I've been able to do for her. She's a darling."

"We're so proud of her," beamed Mrs. Allen, and turned to present the other women. They smiled warmly at Ann and welcomed her into their group as they moved up the aisle and into the big recreation room where a reception was being held for all the brand-new student nurses and their friends and relatives.

Ann looked up when the reception was under way, and her heart gave a small leap as she saw David Lochran standing in the doorway, his eyes scanning the crowded room. She took an impulsive step toward him, and just as she did so, she saw Julia slip from a group of senior nurses and saw the smile he gave her as she tucked her hand through his arm and they went out together.

Ann stood very still for a moment, then scolded herself furiously. What right had she to be disappointed that David had been looking for Julia, not for her, Ann Galt? After all, he had been merely kind to her in taking her to the Hanson concert to fill in when Julia had had to break their date. He had danced with her at the monthly parties just as he had danced with Jessie and the others. Was that any reason he should hunt her up now just to wish her luck? But no matter how she scolded herself, her disappointment persisted.

Jessie had warned Ann that the months immediately following their acceptance as student nurses would be harder than the pre-clinical period, which had consisted mainly of class and laboratory work and a few hours in the wards. And in the weeks that followed they found the warning had been only too true.

Ann's first night duty was a frightening time. The long corridors were deserted, save for a hurrying interne, a staff doctor summoned for an emergency or a nurse moving on swift silent feet to answer the need of a patient.

The R.N.'s in charge of night duty could, Ann discovered, find a terrific number of errands for a first year student to perform. Rarely was she allowed to minister to a patient, since the patients were all asleep at that time; if there was an emergency, a resident, nurse, interne or staff doctor was in attendance and there was little need for a student nurse. But she watched and listened and ran her errands and did what was demanded of her and staggered back to her room to bed, completely exhausted. Since she and Jessie rarely did night duty at the same time, they usually met just as Ann was coming off duty, Jessie going on.

Jessie was marking off the days on the calendar that hung above her bed, yearning for the time when her vacation would begin. And Ann was equally eager.

She had written Clarita about her impulsive invitation to David and Julia to accompany her home for vacation, and Clarita had written to second the invitation. But until a week before the vacation period for the two girls began, Ann was not sure whether the offer would be accepted.

Julia was getting ready for her graduation and the acquisition of her R.N. degree and pin. And David was working very hard to complete his residency to the complete satisfaction of the hospital board that would tell him whether or not he was free to hang up his shingle as an M.D. The final examination at the state capital was also very much in the forefront of his mind.

But eventually, a week before Ann's vacation was due to begin, Julia came over to her in the cafeteria. As she unloaded her tray, she beamed happily at Ann.

"Well, Ann, just another week to go!" She smiled. "And then home to that wonderful Cay!"

"I do hope you'll be able to come with me, Miss Anderson," said Ann politely.

"Oh, I'm going to, thanks a lot," Julia answered. "I've

just discovered that I graduate three days before. The grades have been posted, and I made it! So if you still want me, I'm looking forward to it."

"Of course I want you, and I'm looking forward to it, too," Ann assured her.

"That's fine, then!" said Julia, and added as an afterthought, "Oh, I suppose David has told you he'll be able to come along?"

Ann felt her face grow warm, knew that she was blushing and hated herself for it.

"I'm very glad," she managed. "No, I haven't seen him recently."

"You were both on night duty in Pediatrics, weren't you?" asked Julia.

"Were we? I didn't see him," Ann answered, and made a rueful grimace. "Eleven P.M. until seven A.M. isn't the best time in the world for private conversation, especially in Pediatrics."

"I suppose not," Julia agreed and, for some reason Ann could not quite grasp, seemed relieved. "Well, I saw him at breakfast this morning as he was coming off duty, and he was quite excited about the trip. He thought your great-grandmother's letter was charming, and so did I. She must be a lovely person."

"She is," Ann answered. "And the Cay is just about the most beautiful spot you ever saw."

"I can scarcely wait to see it," Julia answered, and stood up. "Well, I have to rush. I've got eight hours off duty, and I have to do some shopping. Sleeping doesn't seem terribly important at the moment. I suppose I'll need summer things on the Cay?"

"Oh, yes, I'm afraid it will be terribly hot," Ann told her. "I practically live in shorts and bathing clothes except in the evening, and then a thin cotton frock is fine. There's not much entertainment on the Cay. Of course Tad will take us over to Port-au-Prince any time we want to go night-clubbing or shopping."

"I can't think of anything that would interest me less than nightclubbing on your lovely Cay, or leaving it long enough to go shopping anywhere else." Julia smiled at her. "I'll pick up some shorts and a bathing suit then. See you later."

Ann watched her as she moved swiftly across the room

and out into the lobby. And was still watching the spot where she had vanished when Jessie sat down beside her and put her food on the table that a busy attendant had just cleared.

"Julia Anderson and Dr. Lochran are going to the Cay with me," Ann announced, and Jessie stared at her, wide-eyed.

"You're kidding!" she protested.

"I am not! I've been telling you all along that Clarita had written and asked them down."

"Sure, I know. Only somehow I just didn't think they'd go," Jessie admitted frankly. "Don't rustle your bustle, honey, but I didn't know you 'rated' like that with them."

"They are going because they are both tired and want a different kind of vacation and because Clarita asked them; not because of any affection they feel for me," Ann said sharply.

Jessie was round-eyed with surprise. "Well, hey, climb down off that high horse before he throws you!" she urged. "I was just surprised, that's all. I wasn't throwing rocks at you or your precious Cay."

Ann relaxed and touched Jessie's hand in a brief, conciliatory pat. "Sorry. I guess I'm tired, and so homesick I don't see how I can stand three more days of waiting. I wish you were coming, too, Jessie."

"Thanks a whole heap, pal." Jessie shook her head firmly. "Three weeks at home with the family and the gang may not be a key to Paradise, but it sure seems like one! Maybe I can get to the Cay some other time. Maybe after you get to be head nurse down there you may need a good, sound right-hand assistant; and after I get through my commitments to the church circle as a county nurse, I can take a run down there and look things over."

"It's a deal." Ann laughed, and the two girls shook hands.

The day before that set for their departure, Ann received an envelope with the return address of the airline that made a direct flight to Port-au-Prince. Inside it were three round-trip tickets to Port-au-Prince, with a covering letter saying that in accordance with instructions from the *Señora* Galt, of Spanish Cay, three tickets were being enclosed for a flight that would leave the following midnight.

Ann put the tickets in her purse and went on duty. Later, as she came down the corridor, a brisk young man in a white coat and trousers came toward her, and her heart gave a happy leap before she could shush it and tell it to behave itself.

"Good afternoon, Doctor," she greeted him demurely.

"Afternoon, Nurse," said David, took a second look and slowed. "Hey, I didn't recognize you for a moment. After the pink uniform and the big white apron, now you're all done up in blue with a bibbed apron and a cap, yet! Very becoming, too."

"Thank you, Doctor," said Ann, and smothered a pang that in less than three months he had forgotten that she had been promoted. "Miss Anderson says that you are going to be able to accept Clarita's invitation to visit the Cay on your vacation."

"I meant to tell you so myself tonight," David protested. "You must think me very rude and ungracious not to have told you personally, but I haven't been quite positive. I sent your great-grandmother a cable as soon as I got news from Administration that I'm going to be a free man by then."

"Clarita will be glad to know you and Miss Anderson are coming," Ann told him. "The tickets came just now, and we have to be at the airport an hour before midnight. I suppose she ordered the tickets as soon as she got your cable."

David looked mildly startled.

"You mean she's sent tickets for all three of us?" he demanded.

"Well, of course," Ann answered, puzzled at the question.

"Now that seems to be a little too much," David protested. "I'm quite sure Julia and I can pay our own transportation."

"Clarita wouldn't think of allowing that," Ann told him. "From the moment you step aboard the plane at the airport until the moment you leave the return plane you will be her guest. Clarita has some pretty rigid rules of hospitality that she insists be followed to the letter. She'd no more think of allowing you and Miss Anderson to pay your own plane fare than she'd allow you to pay for a meal at the hacienda."

"The more I hear of her the more anxious I am to meet her," said David.

"It's all I can do to wait until we see her again! I've missed her so much!" Ann's voice shook a little, and then she forced a bright, completely unconvincing smile. "Sorry. Nurses don't cry, do they?"

"Well, they aren't supposed to, but now and then I think a few tears should be permissible," David comforted her.

"It's been a lot more than 'a few' for me," Ann confessed humbly. "I've all but been a wet mop of tears most of the time I've been here. But after three weeks with Clarita, I'll brace up and be as stern as Miss Marshall."

She caught her breath as the name slipped out, and her eyes widened in dismay as she met David's.

"I'm sorry," she stammered. "I shouldn't have said that. I didn't mean to criticize Miss Marshall. It's just that she terrifies me."

David laughed and leaned closer, dropping his voice to the tone of a conspirator.

"I'll let you in on a secret," he confided. "She terrifies all of us."

Wide-eyed, Ann protested, "Oh, not you, Doctor! Surely you aren't afraid of her?"

"Petrified!" David insisted firmly. "You know why? She is the very highest echelon of the staff and it ill-behooves a lowly resident not to jump when she speaks."

He sobered almost immediately, and when he spoke again his voice was warm.

"But even while we are all terrified of her, we admire and respect her immensely and feel very, very sorry for her."

Ann gasped and repeated, "Sorry for her?"

David nodded. "Hers is a tough job: being a stern disciplinarian, upholding the dignity and the responsibility of her profession and seeing to it that all who come under her authority do the same. I am sure that there are many, many times when she would like to alter certain rules and regulations; make an exception for some girl; allow the girl to stay in the school even when she has not quite made the grade, either professionally or otherwise. But because of the demands of the nursing profession, she has to be hard as nails. I am sure she does a lot of agonized soul-searching before she reaches the decisions that she has to make. Therefore I am sorry for her."

Ann hesitated, then nodded and said reluctantly, "I suppose you are right."

David laughed and said with mock sternness, "Well, of course I'm right. I'm the doctor, Nurse—remember?"

Ann laughed and made the tiniest mock curtsy.

"But of course, Doctor. How could I ever forget?"

David eyed her for a moment and then said briskly, "Well, I'll see you at the airport tomorrow night."

"Yes, Doctor," said Ann demurely before he went on his brisk way.

Chapter Eight

Twenty-four hours later the three of them stood on the dock at Aux Cayes, the southernmost tip of Haiti, watching a tiny bobbing thing that danced toward them across the incredibly blue Caribbean. All about them lined up against the docks were freighters—some of them rust-stained "tramps"; one of them an impressive-looking ship whose passengers lined the decks watching eagerly as the freight was carried aboard.

David and Julia were as intrigued as the freighter passengers as they watched the colorful scene beneath a bright, hot sun.

Along the edge of the dock, two-wheeled ox-carts swayed into position and natives climbed down and heaved out great sacks of coffee that they had grown on their own tiny farms. A stern-faced white man very carefully inspected each sack and had the contents transferred into a vast container from which other workers were shovelling it into sacks that seemed identical with the original ones. A loud protest broke out after one sack had been weighed; and the white man held up several large rocks that the original sack had held, whereupon the protest broke up in good-natured laughter.

David, watching the transaction, turned to Ann.

"That seems like a lot of extra trouble, transferring the

coffee from one sack to another. Why does the superintendent do it?" he asked curiously.

"Oh, some of the peasants who raise their own coffee and bring it here for sale think it's smart to tuck in a few rocks because it will weigh so much more. They are paid by weight, of course," she explained. "If they can get away with it, fine. But if Mr. McIlvaney catches them, they just think it's a good joke. Mr. Mac found it out a long time ago, so now he insists that every sack be weighed in its original container and then emptied out so he can check on the rocks and then re-weigh it."

"Chicanery even here?" David grinned.

"Why not?" Ann shrugged. "After all, they are people. Basically, I suppose they still consider the white people their enemies, and feel if they can put something over on them they've gained a victory. But they're really fine people. They just ask that we treat them as they are expected to treat us; with dignity and respect and courtesy."

"That doesn't seem a whole lot to ask, now that you point it out," David agreed slowly, and watched with deepened interest as an ox-cart rolled ponderously into its assigned position and the driver, accompanied by a plump wife and several bright-eyed, laughing children, slid to the ground and hefted the first sack of coffee on the scales.

At that moment Ann gave a little cry and ran down to the edge of the dock where a cabin cruiser was warping into a berth that was waiting for it. A tall, sun-tanned young man leaped from the deck up to the dock, and Ann, crying, "Tad! Oh, Tad—am I ever glad to see you!" hurled herself into his welcoming arms.

For a moment they clung and chattered. Then Ann remembered her guests and turned, still holding Tad's hand, and said eagerly, "Julia, Doctor, this is Tad Delehenty. Tad, these are my friends, Dr. Lochran and Miss Anderson."

Tad shook hands with them, grinning.

"This is a very great pleasure, Doctor, Miss Anderson!" said Tad. "And thanks for bringing our girl back to us. She's been sadly missed!"

"Well, who was it that drove me off, I'd like to know?" Ann sniffed. "I didn't want to go, remember? It would serve you right, all of you, if I'd just forgotten to come back."

Tad put his arm about her and drew her close in an impulsive hug even as he laughed down at her.

"Oh, we knew you'd come back," he told her. "The Cay's got a grip on you, and you'll never be happy anywhere else."

"I'm afraid that's painfully true," Ann admitted so seriously that the other looked at her swiftly, before she rallied and demanded eagerly, "Oh, Tad, how's Clarita?"

"She's fine," Tad answered heartily.

Ann eyed him suspiciously.

"Is she really? You're not just saying that?"

Tad stared at her, affronted.

"Now what kind of a question is that? Have I ever lied to you?"

"Oh, *have* you?" Ann sniffed. "Always, of course, with the thought it was for my own good. But don't you dare tell me Clarita is fine if she isn't."

"She's been in a tizzy ever since she got your cable that you were on your way," Tad told her firmly. "She was up at five o'clock this morning making those little petits fours that you're so crazy about! Insisted nobody else, not even Mother, could make them just the way you like them. Would she be doing that if she wasn't fine?"

"Well, yes, she would, for my homecoming," Ann said firmly, and led the way to the cruiser. "Come on; let's get going. I can't wait to see her."

Tad and David stowed the luggage while the two girls stepped aboard and settled themselves. Then Tad cast off, touched the engine, which roared obediently, turned in a sharp, tight circle and set the cruiser speeding back the way it had come.

There was no chance for conversation above the roar of the engine and David and Julia sat entranced as the cruiser sped through the blue waters. Ann sat leaning forward eagerly, straining her eyes for the first sight of her beloved Cay.

The pier thrust out into the water far enough to allow an odd-looking small freighter to tie up to it. Tad sent the cruiser on to a spot closer to the village. Practically the entire population clustered at the end of the pier, waiting. As Ann stepped ashore a great cheer of welcome rang out. As she ran forward, some of the natives came to meet her, and she was engulfed in a tumultuous welcome that made David and Julia and Tad stand back.

"All the workers were given a holiday because she was coming home," Tad explained to David and Julia. "They're crazy about her, and she loves them. It was a shame that she had to be sent away for so long; but Clarita had given up hope of being able to persuade a doctor to replace Dr. John, and she felt the natives had to have medical protection."

"Well, Ann will certainly give it to them," David said quietly. "She's going to make a wonderful nurse. She works very hard."

Tad smiled and nodded. "Went into it headlong, I know, as she does with everything she tackles, once she's convinced it's the right thing to do. She's quite a gal."

Ann, a tiny two-year-old child in her arms, turned to them, laughing.

"Will you look at this creature?" she asked joyously. "When I went away he wasn't much bigger than your fist, and he cried all the time and didn't like anybody. Now look how fat and sleek and sassy he is!"

The little boy's mother beamed and said something which Ann answered in her own patois. The little boy eyed Ann shyly, and Ann hugged him and handed him back to his mother.

"Come on, everybody; don't be slowpokes! Clarita's waiting!" She urged them toward the jeep.

David and Tad saw to the stowing of the luggage which some of the natives had brought from the cruiser, and as the welcoming crowd stood back, waving and shouting after them, the jeep sped through the village and out to the narrow, winding trail that led up to the hacienda. On the way, they passed several ox-carts loaded with sugar cane, making their slow, ponderous way down to the village. Each driver threw up an arm and shouted a greeting as the jeep passed them.

"It's quite obvious," David said from the back seat where he sat with Julia, "that you don't have any racial trouble here at the Cay."

Ann turned to stare at him, wide-eyed and shocked. "Racial trouble?" she repeated incredulously. "Why, these are people, our people! The Cay belongs to them as much as to us. Golly goodness, we're family, aren't we, Tad?"

"Sure we are." Tad grinned at her.

"The Cay could never have been anything but a barren waste without these people," Ann explained as though a little ashamed of her startled outburst. "They've always been made to feel that this is a partnership; not that they are slaves! They receive a percentage of all the Cay produces, and are cared for and loved and protected! I hate to think what would happen if Clarita found one of them was dissatisfied or had been mistreated. They are free to leave if they want to; but not one of them ever leaves."

The jeep had climbed the steep, tortuous trail, and now the hacienda loomed before them, crowning the topmost elevation of the Cay: a big, solid coquina-rock building in the Spanish style, with a wide unscreened terrace at the back that gave what Julia knew must be a breathtaking view of the whole Cay and the blue Caribbean beyond.

As the jeep came to a halt, a woman appeared at the porte-cochère, and Ann cried, "Oh, Mary darling, I'm so glad to see you!"

The two embraced warmly, and then in the doorway a figure appeared that made Julia draw a deep breath of delight. Against the setting of this old Spanish hacienda in its bower of blossoming tropical foliage and shrubbery, the woman was so perfect that for a moment Julia could scarcely make herself believe she was real. Her snowy hair was capped by a black lace mantilla held high at the back with a carved golden comb; her black satin dress was cut in an ancient style, but the quality of the material was so perfect that it seemed to flow about the small, proudly held body.

Ann caught her breath, detached herself from Mary's arms, and folded Clarita close. Clarita held her as though she had been a child and, across her shoulder, smiled at Julia and David.

"You are most welcome, my dears," she said. "I am so very happy you could come. I hope you will enjoy your stay and make it as long as you can."

"You're very gracious," said Julia, and asked, "What do I call you? Ann always says, 'Clarita,' but I don't want to take liberties."

Clarita said gently, "I am Clarita to my friends, my dear. And you are my girl's friend, which makes you my friend. You're Julia, of course, Ann's 'Big Sister.' Welcome to the Cay."

Ann was so moved she could not speak. But Clarita was more than equal to the occasion.

"And you're David," she said, held out a frail hand and gave him a warm smile so like Ann's that he was startled. "Ann has written me so much about you that you are already firmly established in my affections. I'm most grateful for your kindness to her."

"It was a privilege, Clarita," David answered. "Being kind to Ann is no chore at all. In fact, it might even become habit-forming in time."

Tad and two white-coated house boys were bringing in the luggage, and Mary was showing them where it should go. After a moment Ann mastered herself enough to turn and say, her eyes swimming, "I'm ashamed of being such a dope. Only it seemed I hadn't seen Clarita or the Cay or anybody since—oh, for years! I know you want to go to your rooms. Mary darling, will you show them? I've got to check upon Clarita and get all the newest gossip and scandal."

"Of course, darling," said Mary.

With Clarita leaning heavily on her thick cane, and Ann supporting her on the other side, they moved across the wide hall and out to the terrace beyond the living room. Julia and David followed Mary up the stairs, Tad assuring them he would see them at dinner time.

As the three of them moved up the wide, gracious stairs, Mary said over her shoulder, "Ann and Tad have been like brother and sister since they were babies. Tad's missed her desperately this year."

"Not any more than she's missed him and, I'm sure, all of you," Julia said. "And now that I've seen this lovely place I don't wonder she wouldn't want to leave it even for a few weeks, much less for three years."

Mary turned in the vast hall and asked them both, her tone anxious, "She *is* going to make a fine nurse, isn't she?"

David said quickly, "She's going to be one of the best, a truly dedicated nurse."

"I'm so glad, because we are going to need someone very badly," said Mary. "Dr. John is failing badly. But then he works so hard, poor man, and he isn't young by any means."

She broke off to open a door and stand back, smiling at David.

"You're in here, Doctor. And this is Peter, who will valet you while you are here."

The tall, thin young Negro in the spotless white coat straightened and gave David an appealing smile.

"I glad you here, *Señor*," he began in his soft voice.

"English, Peter—remember? The *Señora* insists!" Mary reminded him.

"Yes, of course; I forget. I glad you here, Doctor."

"Well, thanks, Peter. I've never had a valet before, so you may have to instruct me in what you expect of me." David laughed.

Peter looked anxiously at him and then at Mary.

"Don't worry, Peter," Mary soothed him. "Dr. Lochran was making a little joke."

Peter's ebony-hued face split in a white-toothed smile, and he slapped his thigh appreciatively and whooped with laughter.

David protested, "Oh, come Peter. It wasn't that funny!"

Anxiously Peter asked, "What not?"

"Was not," David answered firmly.

He grinned, and Peter's anxiety vanished and he drew a deep, relieved breath.

Mary responded to David's smile and turned to Julia.

"You're here across the hall, Miss Anderson." She indicated a door that stood open, revealing a bed-chamber as huge and as luxuriously furnished as was David's.

A girl in a neat uniform, her face copper-colored, stood at the foot of the vast four-poster bed, Julia's suitcases open before her on a small stand.

"Francesca, this is Miss Anderson," Mary told her. "See that you take good care of her and do as she tells you."

"Oh, yes, Miss Mary."

"Hello, Francesca," said Julia. "I'm sure we're going to be very good friends."

"Thank you, Miss Anderson."

Mary said briskly, "She'll unpack for you, Miss Anderson, and do any pressing that you may need. I'll run along now and see about dinner. Would you care for something to eat, perhaps? Dinner is at seven, and there will be tea in the drawing room at five. You may come down or not, as you like. In fact, you are to do whatever you like while you are here."

"You're more than kind," Julia told her. "No, I wouldn't care for anything at the moment, but I will be down for tea, thank you."

"Good! We'll expect you," said Mary, and smiled as she went out and closed the door behind her.

Chapter Nine

Ann stood at the parapet of the terrace overlooking the sheer drop to the beach and flung out her arms in a gesture that would have embraced the entire scene. Her head flung back, she looked up at the deep-blue sky and then down at the water that rolled in and died on the yellow beach, leaving a white lace of foam.

Clarita, sitting in her special chair beside the low table, strewn with books and magazines and decorated with a low bowl of native orchids, watched her.

"If you could only know how I've missed all this!" she murmured barely above her breath. And then in a slightly louder tone, "But not a tenth as much as I've missed you, darling."

"And I've missed you, my dearest," said Clarita gently, and held out her hand.

Ann came and sat at her feet on a low hassock and cradled Clarita's hand against her cheek.

"Was it so very bad, dear?" asked Clarita at last when Ann seemed in no hurry to speak.

"The homesickness? Terrible!"

"I didn't mean that, dear. I meant the training, the work of becoming a nurse."

"Oh, that," Ann scoffed. "That was a breeze."

Clarita's thin mouth curled in a faint smile.

"I can imagine!" she drawled. "I hated sending you

away, dear, but I could see no other way to provide our people with what they must have."

"Oh, sure," Ann answered carelessly. "We've been all over that, and I'm completely resigned to two more years to go. It's just that I'm so darned glad to be back."

Clarita laughed softly and bent to drop a kiss on the girl's head.

"And I'm so darned glad to have you back," she said warmly.

Ann looked up at her in pretended shock.

"Why, Clarita, you said a bad word!"

"Why, so I did. But that's because you said it first!"

They both laughed, and then Ann looked away again. After a moment she asked with elaborate casualness, "What do you think of David?"

"David?"

"Dr. Lochran, lamb! Isn't he wonderful?" Ann's tone betrayed her, and Clarita's eyes sharpened, though she spoke in a tone as casual as Ann's had been.

"Why, I barely saw the man, but he seems quite handsome."

"Handsome? Darling, he's beautiful!" Ann insisted, and lifted her young face to meet Clarita's eyes. "I like him an awful lot, Clarita. And I think he likes me."

"He's still a resident at the hospital?"

"Oh, no, he's finished his residency, and now he's free to go anywhere he wants to practice as a doctor," Ann answered. There was a rush of color to her face. "Wouldn't it be wonderful if we could get him so interested in the Cay that he would be willing to take over from Dr. John and live here permanently?"

Clarita's brows drew together in a little frown.

"But, darling, do you think that's possible?" she asked slowly.

"Well, I don't know what his plans are," Ann admitted frankly. "He hasn't mentioned any. I imagine he's talked them over with Julia. They're very good friends and have known each other for a long time."

Clarita hesitated for a moment, and then she said gently, "My dearest, we must remember that there are not many opportunities for ambitious young doctors at the Cay. That's why it's been impossible for us to find one who was willing to stay here."

Ann asked quietly, "But what if David asked me to marry him?"

Clarita asked, startled, "Has he?"

"Well, no," Ann responded. "But I'm working on it."

Clarita protested, "Ann, dear!"

"Well, if he falls in love with me and wants to marry me, he'll have to stay at the Cay, because he knows I'd never be willing to live anywhere else."

"Ann, my dear, you're being ridiculous," Clarita told her. "You're talking like an idiot. You're not the reigning monarch of some foreign country who must deny your heart and make a state marriage for the good of your country."

"No?" asked Ann softly. "But if I fell in love with him, Clarita, and he loved me and I really wanted to marry him, you wouldn't try to stop us?"

Clarita studied her shrewdly for a moment, and then she smiled.

"Is this what you thought I sent you away to do? To snare some eligible, attractive young doctor and trap him into life-long servitude at the Cay?" she mocked. But her eyes held a troubled expression.

"Well, wasn't it?" demanded Ann and saw a faint tinge of pink color Clarita's wrinkled face.

"Of course not, you foolish child!" Clarita scolded.

Ann studied her sharply.

"Sure?"

"Don't be impertinent, Ann. Of course I'm sure. Such cold-blooded—"

Ann said quietly, "Well, it wouldn't be cold-blooded if we fell in love. And I don't think that's going to be a bit hard to do, now that I've got him away from the hospital where we can be alone and where I can convince him that the Cay is just about the most beautiful place in all the world."

From the living room they heard voices. David and Julia came out on the terrace, and Ann scrambled to her feet. Her eyes swept over Julia in a thin, cool cotton dress of pale yellow and white stripes, a thin yellow sweater swung about her shoulders. Above the pale yellow her hair was sleek and shining in the sunset light, her brown-gold eyes taking in the scene about her with lively enjoyment.

"What a gorgeous view!" she exclaimed as she walked

to the waist-high parapet, looked down the rocky drop to the beach and drew back with a slight gasp. "Heavens, what a drop!"

"That's why the parapet is so high," Ann explained. "Does it make you dizzy to look down? Then come over here and look at the coffee plantation. It doesn't drop; it slopes! That's why the coffee is the best in the world."

Clarita laughed up at David, who was watching the two girls with an amused glint in his eyes.

"Our Ann is modest about her own accomplishments, but when she mentions the Cay's products, she has no shame!" she teased.

"Well, it *is* good coffee; else why do we get a better price for it than other plantations around?" Ann defended herself, and indicated to Julia the terraces that curved above the small village.

"It's a fabulous place!" David said as he joined the two girls. "Ann, I don't wonder you hated leaving it, even to become a nurse. But the memory of this should see you through the next two years before you can come back to stay for the rest of your life."

Ann looked up at him and asked quietly, "Do you think so?"

Mary came out on the terrace, followed by a house man rolling an amply laden tea wagon which he placed before Clarita.

Ann said briskly, "I'd better run up and change for dinner," and added to Julia, "You look lovely, Julia."

Before Julia could answer, Ann asked, "It's all right for me to call you Julia away from the hospital, isn't it?"

"Of course it is," Julia answered.

Ann turned brightly to David and said, "And I don't have to keep on saying, 'Yes, Doctor,' do I? Now I can say, 'No, David,' if I want to?"

David laughed. "Just so long as you don't forget when you get back to the hospital. But then of course I won't be there when you get back. I've finished my residency, and now I'm out in the 'cold, crool world' on my own!"

Clarita said, "But I'm sure you must have some carefully laid plans to warm that world, David?"

David smiled down at her. "They are so vague and unsettled at present I don't dare talk about them," he answered.

Julia cut in with a pleasant, "But I'm sure whatever he does, David will be very good at it."

Her eyes met Ann's and locked. Then Ann, her mouth a thin set line, turned and left the terrace. Behind her she heard the pleasant rattle of thin silver and even thinner china and the voices of David and Clarita and Julia as she hurried up the stairs and to her own quarters.

She went through the rack of things that she had used at the Cay until she found a sheer jade-green organdie with a snugly fitted bodice and a ballerina-length very full skirt that swirled above her ankles. High-heeled silver-strapped sandals, stockings so sheer that they seemed non-existent, her hair piled high on her head—and the result was something she eyed with frank approval.

That, she told herself as she touched the stopper of the tall perfume bottle to the backs of her ears and along the inner curve of her elbow, ought to give Julia a run for her money and help David make up his mind about where he wants to practice.

She came down the stairs to find that Tad and Dr. John had joined the party on the terrace and were staying for dinner. Tad was talking to Julia with every evidence of enjoying the conversation immensely. But when Ann came out on the terrace he broke off in mid-sentence, jumped to his feet and came to greet her, his eyes shining with delight.

"Look what she's done, Dr. John," he said over his shoulder, smiling accusingly at Ann. "She went away and grew up on us. You think she's the same girl we saw off?"

Dr. John turned an affectionate smile on her and held out his hands.

"She's the same girl, Tad, my boy," he answered as Ann bent and brushed her lips against his cheek. "She's just gotten more beautiful when she was away and a year older. But haven't we all? Grown older, I mean."

"Phooey!" retorted Ann inelegantly. "You're younger than springtime, Dr. John. You and Clarita are like fine old wine; you just improve as the years go by."

Dr. John's eyes twinkled at David, who was lounging against the parapet, his arms folded, watching the scene with interest.

"I hope you've taught her as much about her profession as you have about wielding a flattery-brush," Dr. John said.

"Oh, she's learning fast!" David laughed. "She rises instantly when a doctor enters the room."

"Well, I should hope so!" Dr. John seemed scandalized at the bare thought that she might not.

"And she's got a way with the convalescent patients that is a beautiful thing to see, and the kids in Pediatrics adore her," David finished.

"Well, wasn't that what you expected of me when you persuaded Clarita to throw me out into that cold crool world David was talking about?" Ann demanded.

"Nobody threw you out," Dr. John protested.

"And I do hope she didn't find the training school too cold or cruel," said Julia smoothly. "I drew her name as her Big Sister and did everything I could to smooth the way for her."

Ann flickered a glance in her direction and said sweetly, "Oh, it wasn't so bad. And you were most kind."

"I tried to be," Julia answered.

David glanced from one to the other of the lovely young faces, and a tiny wrinkle of bewilderment touched his forehead. The words of the two girls were irreproachable; but was there just possibly the faintest tinge of acid in their tone?

They had dinner, and the evening passed.

It was Dr. John who stood up at last and, with an anxious look at Clarita, said briskly, "Well, I think we'd better break up this lovely party. Clarita looks very tired, and I'm sure you would all like to get to bed."

He crossed to Clarita and took her frail hand, his fingers unobtrusively searching for her pulse.

"Now, John, don't fuss!" Clarita protested.

"While David is here, Clarita, I wish you'd let him give you a thorough physical," Dr. John began.

"Nonsense!" Clarita's voice was stronger now. "That's an outrageous suggestion! Dr. Lochran is here on a holiday. We're certainly not going to ask him to sing for his supper."

"I'd be very happy to be of any possible service," David insisted.

"We're wasting our time on her, David," Dr. John

sighed. "She maintains she is the healthiest critter on the Cay."

"My only disease," stated Clarita firmly, "is one that not even the most inspired and dedicated doctors can heal. It's known as old age."

David said quickly, with a smile, "Medicine is doing such marvelous things nowadays in the study of geriatrics."

Clarita's smile was very faint.

"So I've heard," she told him, and her voice was unexpectedly sober. "You can prolong life, I know, David. But can you prolong the will to live? Are you so sure you're doing old people a service by maintaining lives that must long ago have become dull and dreary and painfully lonely?"

"Clarita!" It was Ann crying out against the inescapable logic of Clarita's words.

Clarita put up a frail hand, and Ann's warm young ones closed eagerly over it. Clarita's smile was tender.

"Oh, don't worry, darling," she said. "Dr. John and I will still be right here waiting for you when you complete your training."

"Well, you'd better be!" Ann sniffed to hold back the tears. "It wouldn't be the Cay without you two."

"Oh, yes, it would," Clarita corrected her. "The Cay has been here for hundreds of years. It will be here for many, many more."

"But without you here, I wouldn't want to come back, ever," Ann insisted.

"Of course you would, darling!" Clarita told her, and turned to her guests. "Dear me, what a lugubrious note on which to end your first night at the Cay. I am truly sorry!"

"It's been a wonderful night," said Julia. "And you are more than kind to let us stay here. Isn't she, David?"

She turned her head, and the smile she gave David brought him to her side to stand looking down at Clarita. Ann, watching the two of them side by side, felt a small pang in her heart.

She turned away to walk with Tad and Dr. John out to their cars.

Dr. John kissed her cheek lightly, got into his jeep and drove away. For a long moment Tad and Ann stood at the edge of the drive, looking out over the steep sweep of lawn and shrubbery and the tall palms that seemed to brush the sky. A full moon sailed serenely overhead and spilled a bright wash of silver-white over the scene; the ink-black shadows beneath the trees made a brilliant mosaic. The air was fragrant with the scent of tropical blooms faintly tinged with the salty tang of the sea that tiptoed through the tops of the palms.

Ann stood in a deep silence, savoring the scene before her, until at last Tad asked gently, "Glad to be home, Annie, my girl?"

"I would be," Ann told him huskily, "if I didn't know that I'd have to leave again for another whole year. Oh, Tad, I don't want to go back!"

"I don't want you to, honey." Tad took her in his arms as though she had been a grieving child. "But we know how much Clarita has set her heart on it. I'm afraid you'll have to go, honey."

Ann nodded, resting her head against his shoulder.

"I know," she answered. "It's got to be done. I have to do it. But I don't have to like it."

Tad laughed softly. "That you don't, my pretty. I guess as long as you do it, nobody can quarrel if you don't like it."

There was a silence for a moment, and then she drew herself from his arms and her grin was impish.

"Maybe if I keep going away and then coming back you might some day find out that you like having me here," she teased him.

"Now what kind of an idiotic remark is that? Have I ever *not* liked having you here?" he demanded.

Ann laughed and patted his cheek lightly and said briskly, "Now run along and get your sleep. You'll have to be all bright-eyed and bushy-tailed come morning, and I've been taught less than eight hours sleep isn't good for busy little boys!"

"Nor for little girls," Tad told her. "And there are times when I feel you can't be more than five years old. See you tomorrow."

She stood and watched until the red glimmer of the tail light on the jeep twinkled out of sight around a curve in the steep trail before she turned and went back into the house.

Chapter Ten

Ann spent the first week at the Cay renewing old friendships with the people with whom she had grown up. She was in and out of the cottages in the village, laughing, gay, warmly interested. Frequently she took Julia with her on these visits, and Julia responded warmly to the shy but eager greetings of the native people.

David and Dr. John had hit it off from their first meeting, and frequently David rode with Dr. John on his rounds. He also spent many hours at the clinic with Dr. John.

Always in the evening Tad was there for dinner, and the four of them then were like any four young people together for relaxation. Clarita sat and watched; her eyes tender on the girl who was the last of the Galts and to whose hands she had to leave the Cay before many more years had passed.

Clarita had no fears about that. The Cay would be in good and loving hands when Ann took over control from her. And there were many times during that first week when she wished with all her heart that she need not send the girl away again. But she knew that she had to, for the good of the Cay and its loyal, devoted, trusting population.

After the first week occupied with renewing old friendships, Ann tardily remembered that this could not be very exciting or entertaining for her guests. And so there were hours on the beach; a picnic high up in the all but inaccessible reaches of the mountains beyond the sugar mill. One day Tad took them in the cabin cruiser across to Aux Cayes, and from there hired a car and drove them on a tour of the country.

"I warned you," Ann told David and Julia as they were returning from the trip, "that there wasn't much excitement or entertainment down here except what we create for ourselves."

David and Julia, in the back seat of the jeep as it struggled valiantly up the narrow trail to the hacienda, laughed in unison.

"Anybody who wanted anything more on a vacation than you've shown us, Ann, would be an unbearably greedy person," Julia said.

"It's by all odds the finest vacation I've ever had or hope to have," David agreed. "Dr. John is a marvelous person and what he's doing down here, his research—it's fantastic! He's become a legend in his own lifetime. It's a privilege to know him."

Ann, sitting beside Tad in the front, turned to beam joyously at him.

"Oh, that's the nicest thing anybody could have said about him," she said happily. "I do hope you've told him that. He'd love hearing it. He thinks he's a rank failure and a dull, stodgy stick-in-the-mud sort of medico."

"He couldn't possibly think such a thing!" David protested. "Any man who does what he is doing is a credit to the medical profession. I don't know any truly dedicated doctor who wouldn't envy him."

Ann's eyes were glowing as she turned back and caught Tad's suddenly intent gaze.

After dinner that night, when Ann walked with Tad out to the jeep, he looked down at her in the silver moonlight and said quietly, "So he's the one."

Ann looked up at him, startled.

"The one?" she repeated.

"Don't be coy with me, young-'un," Tad said. "You know perfectly well what I mean. You left here with the frankly avowed intention of snagging yourself a bright, dedicated young doctor and luring him to the Cay for life even if you had to marry him. Is Lochran the fellow you had in mind?"

Ann disdained to pretend. She raised her chin defiantly and asked coolly, "Any objections?"

"I haven't," Tad told her. "But you may have your work cut out for you. Seems Julia has an eye on the fellow, too."

"You could stop that if you wanted to," Ann said.

Now it was Tad's turn to stare down at her, scowling and bewildered.

"Just what am I supposed to do?"

"Oh, be nice to Julia."

"I have been."

"I know. But I mean a whole lot nicer. For instance, you could flirt with her a bit."

She heard the sharp breath Tad drew even as his hands clamped on her shoulders and shook her.

"Why, you shameless, outrageous little somebody!" His tone told her he was genuinely angry. "I ought to spank the daylights out of you, the way I used to enjoy doing when we were kids and you'd got out of line."

Ann wrenched herself free of his hands and stood out of reach, her head up, her eyes blazing. Even in the silver moonlight he could see the dark color in her face, the gleam of her angry eyes.

"You lay a finger on me, Tad Delehenty, and you'll wish you hadn't," she told him hotly. "All I said was that if I'm trying to snag David—"

"Which you are."

"All right! I don't deny it." Ann told him hotly. "And why not? It's all for the good of the Cay."

"Listen to me, you bird-brain." Tad was genuinely angry now. "Nobody is asking you to sacrifice yourself for the Cay."

"Who said it would be a sacrifice?"

That brought Tad up to his feet. For a moment he studied her in the flower-fragrant, moonlit beauty of the night.

"Are you by any crazy chance trying to tell me you're in love with the guy?" he demanded.

She hesitated for a moment and then answered stubbornly, "I'm not quite sure."

"Then believe me, my girl, it's not love!"

"How can you be so sure? What do you know about love?"

"Very little, I admit," Tad confessed with no trace of humility. "But all I've ever read or heard from people who *do* know is that there is no uncertainty whatever. The minute you fall, you know."

"How?"

"Well, how the blazes should I know? According to popular songs and love stories and the like, it's a sort of Fourth of July inside, with rockets bursting in air, horns blowing and bells ringing."

"Well, if it's like that, I'm not sure I'd like it."

"Nobody asks you to like it, any more than anybody asks you to like an earthquake or a cyclone or a hurricane. It's just something that happens, and you make the best of it."

Ann looked up at him with a faint touch of respect. "For a man who doesn't know anything about love, you seem to have made a very interesting discovery," she said uneasily.

"Oh, well, a fellow has ways of picking up such information," he drawled. "Anyway, you talk to Clarita."

"I have."

"Oh? And what did she say?"

"That I mustn't marry just to get a doctor for the Cay."

"And so you mustn't! Have you talked to Mother?"

"Golly, of course not!"

"You'd better," Tad said quietly. "She can give you just about the best advice of anybody I know about what it's like to fall in love."

"Is that where you got all your knowledge?"

"Some of it," Tad answered cautiously. "You want to know how it came about that she told me what it's like really to love somebody?"

"I'm not sure I'll like it," Ann temporized.

"Which is all the more reason for hearing it," Tad told her. "It was just after you'd gone away last year and I missed you like the dickens. I asked Mother if she thought I was in love with you."

Ann drew a sharp breath.

"And what did she say?" she asked when he showed no inclination to go on.

"She said that I wasn't," Tad informed her.

"Well, thanks a lot!"

"Oh, don't ruffle your feathers!" Tad drawled. "She thought it was only because we'd grown up here together. Neither of us had had an opportunity to know other young people; we were just so accustomed to each other that we could probably make a reasonably good marriage. But she felt we should both wait, because somewhere just ahead there might be the Fourth of July, fireworks, bells and the works."

"And she was so right!" snapped Ann.

"So now you've got a candidate for the Cay's medical staff of one," Tad told her.

"Well, of course he doesn't know it yet."

"And what's the situation in regard to fireworks, rockets and all that fuss-and-feathers?"

Ann hesitated and then said reluctantly, "Well, I like him a lot. I could just as easy as not be really in love with him, if I was sure he was in love with me."

To her outrage, Tad tipped back his head and gave an inelegant hoot of derisive laughter.

"If you were sure!" he repeated. "Infant, let me tip you off to something: you're never sure of anything when you're in love. From all I've heard it's a darned uncomfortable way to be: halfway between Heaven and Hades; sky-high with delight one minute; plunged into the nethermost pits of gloom the next. Your whole existence seems to hinge on the way he looks; the tone of his voice; whether he is present or far away; whether you've quarreled or you've just made up again."

"Well, thank *you*, Professor!" sneered Ann.

"Oh, I'm not speaking from actual experience, you understand."

"I'm sure you're not. Few experts on any subject are."

"Don't get sassy with me, young'un!"

She hesitated a moment, and then she laid a hand on his arm coaxingly.

"Will you help me, Tad dear?" she pleaded.

Tad looked down at her warily.

"Help you with what?"

"Getting a lifetime doctor for the Cay."

Tad looked down at her in the moonlight and wished devoutly that it were mid-day so that he could see her face, her eyes, her expression.

"You're really serious about this?" he demanded.

"Well, of course I am, Tad!" There was the faintest possible quaver in her voice. "Oh, Tad, I don't ever want to leave the Cay again. And with a permanent doctor here I wouldn't have to. Tad, won't you do this for me? It's such a little thing to ask.

"A little thing?" he repeated. "Ann, I think you must have flipped your ever-lovin' lid! I have never heard anything so ridiculous in my life. You ought to be spanked!"

Anger flooded Ann's whole being, and she stepped back and glared up at him.

"What's ridiculous about it? And anyway, I told you before I left a year ago what I hoped to do. And you said you'd help me."

"I said no such thing!"

"Well, you hinted you would. And now that I've worked so hard to get both of them here, all I'm asking you to do is to keep Julia out of my hair long enough for me to convince David he'd be perfectly happy here forever."

"You really think you can do that, don't you?"

"Well, at least I could try, if you'd only help."

There was a brief, taut silence, and then Tad made a gesture of defeat.

"I'm a fool, I know, to fall in with your cockeyed scheme. But Julia is a lovely person, and it would be no hardship whatever for me to pay her devoted attention. And after all, it's only for another couple of weeks."

Ann caught her breath in a little ecstatic gasp and flung herself upon him, her arms embracing him tightly, her cheek pressed hard against his own. And Tad, to keep from being bowled over by the force of her onslaught, put his own arms about her and steadied both of them. She turned her cheek until her lips met his in a frank, enthusiastic kiss that, both to her surprise and his, lingered just a little and wasn't quite the sisterly kiss she had intended. After a moment they drew apart and stared at each other. And then, without a word, Tad turned from her and strode to the jeep.

She watched as the jeep raced at a dangerous pace down to the trail that led to the village before at last she turned and went slowly into the house, looking very thoughtful. . . .

A day or two later Ann and Julia were on the tiny beach below the hacienda; a spot that was enclosed by huge rocks and that offered excellent opportunities for sun-bathing.

Julia, in a snugly fitting white suit, lay face up on a big beach towel, small cotton pads over her closed eyes as she soaked up the sunshine that was already beginning to turn her body into an exquisite pale gold.

Ann, born and raised on the sun-swept Cay so that she had no aching desire to soak up sunshine, sat cross-legged beside her. Her brief sun-suit exposed arms and legs already regaining the warm copper tones they had lost during her year away from the Cay. She was scooping up sand and idly letting it drift through her fingers as she eyed Julia covertly.

"Was there ever such peace, such golden beauty?" Julia sighed at last and removed the pads to look up at Ann, laughing. "I think I'm done on this side. If I roll over on my stomach, will you rub some sun-tan oil into my back? I want to make everybody I know sick with envy when I get back looking like an Indian maiden!"

Ann poured sun-tan oil into her palm and, as Julia rolled over, began massaging it gently into Julia's shoulders, back and legs.

"Will you be going back to Blalock, Julia?" she asked at last.

Julia, half-asleep, said carelessly, "I don't think David has quite decided. I can't, of course, unless he does."

Ann's hand paused in its gentle, slow stroking and her eyes widened. "Oh, your plans are mixed up with David's?"

Julia laughed, a soft, silky laugh that held a wealth of tenderness.

"Of course. Didn't you know?" she asked. "I suppose we must have been even more discreet than we knew. I was afraid we were an 'item' to everybody in the whole place. It's always been like that with David and me. Wherever he goes, whatever he does, I'll be right there beside him. We've both known from the first that that was the way it had to be."

"I didn't know," said Ann huskily, and the hand that was massaging lotion into Julia's back and shoulders was slow and heavy in its ministrations.

Julia sat up and studied her, frowning slightly.

"You really didn't know, Ann?" she asked.

Ann fought hard for a measure of composure that would disguise her shock and disappointment.

"I really didn't, Julia," she managed. "Oh, I think you'd make a perfectly marvelous team, of course. You'd be just about perfect for each other. And I wish you all the happiness in the world."

"Thanks," said Julia, smiling, though her eyes on Ann were shrewd and not untouched with pity. "David's considering a couple of good offers to go in with established medical men with whom he has worked at Blalock. But I think he's even more interested in a plan two of his friends have to open a charity clinic in an isolated rural area in South Georgia. You may have met them; they were both residents this past year. George Holmes and Fayette Mabry. Fayette is from this small rural town. There isn't a hospital within thirty miles, and the county is so thinly populated that they haven't hope of getting a hospital. Fayette feels that a clinic would be a wonderful thing for the area. And he wants David and George to go in with him to establish and operate it."

Ann was still for a moment, and then she asked, "And of course they'll need a good nurse, too?"

Julia laughed. "Well, if David goes, what they'll get as a nurse is me!"

"They'd be in luck, then," Ann told her.

As though talking of David's plans were something she had long wanted to do, Julia went on slowly, "Of course it's the sort of set-up that wouldn't appeal to a great many newly fledged medics. There's very little money and a lot of hard work. But David feels it would be very rewarding. He wants to serve where he is needed, and he feels this could easily be the place."

"And do you feel that way, too?" asked Ann.

Julia laughed and flung out her arms in a happy gesture.

"Whatever David wants is what I want," she said joyously. "I want to make a home for him. The poor darling's never had one. I want to take care of him, make him happy. And doing what he wants to do is the best way to insure his happiness."

She turned to Ann and laid a hand on her knee, her eyes warm and sweet. "This is the most wonderful vacation either of us can ever hope to have, Ann. It put the most gorgeous finish on our years of hard work. David and I will never forget you, the Cay, your lovely great-grandmother, Dr. John and the native people. You've got a wonderful destiny waiting for you here when you finish your training, Ann. To know that all of these people love you and will be dependent on you for their health and welfare must make you very proud and happy."

Ann swallowed hard and managed huskily, "I'll miss you at Blalock."

Julia smiled. "Oh, well, you won't be needing a Big Sister any more. You'll be a student nurse; not a probie. And you can snoot the probies if you like."

Ann shook her head soberly. "I won't want to. I'll know too well how scared and homesick and bewildered they are. I'll want to do everything I can to help them. The first year is the roughest. At least that's what I've been told, and I hope it's true."

"It is, Ann dear," Julia assured her, smiling. "Now that you know the ropes, it will be a breeze."

"Now that I shall hope to see," Ann answered, and scrambled to her feet. "Well, my stomach tells me it must be nearly lunch time. Shall we start making like mountain goats and see if we can get back to the hacienda?"

"Why don't we?" Julia agreed. They started across the beach to the path that led toward the house that crowned the top of the hill.

"If we'd been real smart—" Ann paused, panting for breath, when they were halfway to the top—"we'd have made Tad drive us down to the village in the jeep, and then we could just have walked around."

"But Tad was busy, remember?" Julia said, and added, "He's quite a guy, Ann. I like him very much."

Ann turned swiftly. "Do you?" she asked eagerly.

"Of course I do," Julia answered as though surprised at Ann's tone. "Where did he ever get a name like Tad? It must be a nickname."

Ann nodded as they turned and began climbing once more.

"His name is really Thaddeus," she explained over her shoulder. "He was named for his grandfather, who didn't want Mary to marry the man she fell in love with. Mary promised that if her father would give them his blessing and not make a fuss, they'd name the first son for him. And the grandfather's name was Thaddeus. But when we were little, I couldn't say Thaddeus; he's five years older than I am. The best I could manage was Tad. He liked it, and gradually it became his name, just as Clarita became my great-grandmother's name to everybody on the Cay. No one ever calls her anything but Clarita, and no one ever calls him anything but Tad."

"And what does his grandfather say about that?" Julia wondered as they reached the top of the hill.

"Oh, his grandfather died when Tad was only two, so he never knew that Thaddeus had become Tad," Ann answered. "Oh, fooey! That was quite a climb, wasn't it? And now we'd better step lively if we don't want to keep lunch waiting. Clarita is a stickler for having meals on time."

In her own room, with the door closed tightly, Ann faced the destruction of her eager hopes that she would be able to persuade David to stay on at the Cay. She should have known, she told herself desolately as she showered and changed into a thin, sleeveless sun-dress of cool white, that there was going to be no easy way out for her. She would have to go back to Blalock for two more years before she could return here to stay.

At dinner that night she watched David and Julia and told herself that she had been a blind fool not to have realized from the very first how they felt about each other. That was because, she reminded herself with her usual painfully realistic honesty, she hadn't wanted to see it. She had deliberately blinded herself; David had been kind to her just because she was Julia's little sister.

Clarita's soft voice penetrated her gloomy thoughts, and she looked up with a trace of guilt.

"Aren't you feeling well, dear?" asked Clarita. "You aren't eating anything at all."

"We were on the beach for hours," Julia suggested. "Maybe she got too much sun."

"Phooey!" Ann protested with inelegant gaiety. "That couldn't possibly happen to me. I'm the sun's own child! I could get a touch of gray skies and chill winds in Capitol City, but not a touch of the sun at the Cay!"

"Drop in at my office, Ann," suggested Dr. John. "I'll find something to build up your appetite."

"You wouldn't dare!" Ann protested. "There's nothing even remotely wrong with my appetite! Unless you can give me something to curb it, I'll be as fat as a pig two weeks from now when we'll be leaving."

Clarita's eyes were troubled as she watched the girl. Then Tad spoke up, changing the subject.

"Heard anything about that tropical disturbance that's supposed to be brewing up, Dr. John?" he asked.

"Oh, it will probably blow itself out before it gets this

far," said Dr. John casually. "They usually do this early in the season."

"Well, let's hope so." Clarita smiled at her guests. "We hoped to offer you some entertainment peculiar to the tropics. But we hadn't planned to go as far as a hurricane. Shall we have our coffee in the living room?"

Chapter Eleven

But the hurricane did not blow itself out. For a day or two the sky held a sullen, grayish look, obscuring the sun. The heavy rolling swells reflected its grayness, and the wind increased until the palms bent submissively before it and the lower trees were torn and tossed and the blossoming shrubbery was bent flat.

The radio gave frequent reports of the progress of the storm until at lunch one day Clarita said quietly, "The village must be evacuated."

Ann gasped, "You think we'll be hit, Clarita?"

"I think it's quite possible, darling," said Clarita. To Julia and David she said apologetically, as though the storm were due to some failing of hers as a hostess, "I'm so dreadfully sorry, but I'm really afraid we are in for a rather bad time. It's too bad we didn't face up to the possibility while there was still time for you to leave. Now you'll have to stay."

David said, "You surely don't think we'd leave now, even if we could! Dr. John may need some help if it's really a bad one."

Clarita said quietly, "Dr. John is going to need all the help he can get. We've had these 'blows' at the Cay before, but this one threatens to be one of the worst."

She looked from one to the other and said, "I don't want to frighten you, but I do think you should be warned. I'm afraid it's going to be very unpleasant."

David smiled at her as he stood up. "You just tell us what we should do and we'll be glad to do it."

"Of course we will," said Julia instantly, and rose and stood beside him.

Ann looked from one to the other and felt a pang in her heart. Yes, she told herself forlornly, they were a team. They belonged together, and it was good that that was the way it was going to be.

"I'm sure Dr. John and Tad are already arranging the evacuation," Clarita told them gratefully. "They will have heard the radio reports and will know that, while we haven't too much to fear from the winds, we do have to expect terrifically high tides that will flood the village."

She was almost matter of fact about it, and Julia and David exchanged swift glances.

"Where will the people go?" asked Julia.

Clarita was obviously surprised at the question.

"Why, they will come here, of course," she answered. "Those who can will get to the mill; those who are already there will stay there. The others will come here."

Mary said briskly, "I'll see to the arrangements for them."

"Do we have plenty of food?" asked Clarita anxiously.

"Of course we do, dear, and clothes and blankets. And I'm sure Dr. John has an ample supply of medical necessities at the clinic." Mary smiled comfortingly at her and then at David and Julia. "We're rarely unprepared for such an emergency here. They're not nearly as rare as we would like."

She hurried out, and David turned to Clarita.

"Perhaps I should go down to the clinic and offer my services to Dr. John? That is, if you think he is likely to need me?" David suggested.

"I'm sure he would be most grateful," said Clarita. "The jeep is in the drive. Tad has his at the mill, and Dr. John's will be at the clinic."

"I'll go with you, David," said Julia. "Shall I change into a uniform?"

"I doubt if there will be time," said Clarita quietly, and for the first time they realized that her crumpled old face was pale and her eyes deeply troubled.

"Then we'll leave immediately," said David, and turned toward the door.

"I'd better go, too, don't you think, Clarita?" suggested Ann. "There'll be some that can't walk. I can bring them back here while David and Julia stay at the clinic with Dr. John."

"Of course, dear." Clarita was relieved and managed a faint smile as Ann bent swiftly, brushed the crumpled face with her lips and hurried out after David and Julia.

They had to bend against the wind that screamed and tore at them in savage fury as they struggled across the drive and all but fell into the car. The wind seemed determined to fling them over the cliff down to the beach. Under its fury the palms bent and swayed like frightened creatures, and the steep lawn was already thick with blossoms torn from the shrubbery. The sky was gray and boiling with dark clouds. As David sent the jeep down the trail at a speed that he would not have dared under less alarming circumstances, they could feel it rock and sway as the wind clutched at it with savage fingers that fought against being cheated of its prey.

Long before they reached the village they met people streaming up the trail, carrying such of their belongings as they had been able to catch up before they were forced to flee. The big clumsy two-wheeled ox-carts were much in evidence, piled with household belongings. Small, big-eyed children perched atop some of them.

They reached the clinic, and David pulled the jeep to a sharp halt. He and Julia tumbled out and went running into the clinic, while Ann slid beneath the wheel and drove on to the village, which was on a lower level than the clinic.

As the jeep rattled down the street between the double row of cottages, people erupted from doorways and greeted Ann with shouts of relief.

They began bringing out the aged and the infirm, and Ann took as many as she could into the jeep and, after promising to return immediately for more, turned and went racing back up the trail.

As she made her third trip the rain came down in a paralyzing deluge. Driven by the fury of the quickening wind that howled like a demoniac creature, the rain was tipped with icy needles. Soaked within an instant, the sick and infirm in the jeep wailed aloud, and Ann set her teeth hard, blinking the rain out of her eyes as she fought her way up to the top of the hill where eager, loving hands removed her passengers.

Without a word, once the jeep was empty, she turned

to go back. There were a few more left in the village, and she would not abandon them. The thought that she was risking her own life in the perilous journey did not occur to her at all. These were Galt Cay people; they were entitled to everything she or any other Galt could do for them.

Her heart lifted a little when she reached the village and saw Tad's jeep there.

"Why aren't you at the mill?" she demanded breathlessly.

"Why aren't you at the hacienda?" he countered, a grin touching his weary face against which the rain beat with savage force. "McGuire is looking after the refugees at the mill. I came down to see if I could find out where old Mam' Cleo has her hideaway and get her out of it before she drowns."

"Mam' Cleo? The voodoo woman?"

"The same," said Tad grimly. "We've got to find her and bring her in."

"Of course," said Ann without an instant's hesitation. "We'll leave my jeep at the clinic for Julia and David, and we'll go in yours."

"Swell!" Tad answered grimly. "Go where? You know how she hides out and nobody will tell you where she is. Preacher Sam gives sermons criticizing her voodoo and witchcraft. The people are afraid of her, and of Preacher Sam, too. But they're a lot more afraid of her than of him!"

Ann scanned the street ahead of them. Doors stood wide, and only a few chickens and dogs were visible. Obviously the last of the villagers had been evacuated.

"Maybe Dr. John will know," suggested Ann, and turned back to the clinic.

Inside, the place was crowded, although the villagers had all been warned to go to the hacienda. However, there were a few of Dr. John's patients who clung persistently to him and felt that wherever he was, there was safety.

Ann looked swiftly about the room where they waited for his services—the sick, the hurt, the ailing, and the just plain scared.

Dr. John appeared in the door of his tiny surgery room and scanned the group.

"All right," he barked. "Who's next? Ann, what are you and Tad doing here?"

"We have to find Mam' Cleo, Dr. John," Ann began, and an expression of deep disgust touched Dr. John's face.

"That old witch!" he barked.

"Dr. John, stop talking like that. She's a woman and old and feeble, and she's been on the Cay all her life. Surely you know where her hideaway is," Ann protested.

"I don't know a darned thing about the old witch, and the best thing that could happen to the Cay would be for her to drown," snarled Dr. John, and staggered and clung to the door frame.

Instantly Ann was beside him, steadying him. The next moment Julia was there, competent, capable, easing him into a chair as she glanced up at Ann.

"You run along, Ann," she said quietly. "David and I will look after him. There aren't many casualties—yet! Maybe the evacuation was in time after all."

"Oh, this is just the beginning," Tad told her grimly. "The tides are what we have to fear, and the water is rising by the minute. Come on, Ann. We've got to find the old creature."

Outside in the pouring rain driven by the terrific winds, Ann clung to the side of the jeep and looked up at Tad through the streaming rain.

"It's not a very big Cay, Tad," she managed to gasp, "but it's a bit too big for us to dash off in all directions hunting a spot where an old voodoo woman set up shop."

There was a feeble gasp behind her, and she turned to see an incredibly ancient man, his hair white as cotton above his ashen, terror-stricken face as he babbled something.

"The *Señorita*, the *Señor*—they wish to find the *mamaloi?*"

"Do you know where she is, Jabez?" asked Ann.

"You will not harm her?"

"You fool!" Tad raged. "Of course we won't harm her. But the storm will if we don't find her and bring her here."

Swiftly the old man described the place that the old voodoo priestess had claimed for her own.

Tad and Ann looked at each other in shock as the

old man divulged the secret hiding place of the old woman.

"Why, that's that old ravine between the hacienda and the sugar mill," Tad identified the location. "She's probably drowned by now. Come on, Ann. I'll drop you off at the hacienda."

Ann slid into the jeep and said grimly, "You'll do no such thing. I'm going with you."

"Now, Ann—'

"Don't you 'now, Ann' me," snapped Ann, "unless you want me to drive. And believe me, buddy-boy, that could be dangerous. It's been a long time since I've been over that trail."

"What trail?" demanded Tad bitterly. "It's nothing even faintly resembling a trail. You have to wind your way through trees and over brush, and when you get to the top of the ravine you have to be a mountain goat to get down to the beach. And that'll be where the old gal has set up her camp; where there's room for her clients to make whoopee in their own vile way!"

"Well, let's get going," ordered Ann sharply.

Behind them the old man stood in the driving fury of the storm, until a voice summoned him from inside the clinic and he turned reluctantly to go back inside.

The jeep fought its way up toward the sugar mill. About halfway up, Tad turned the jeep in between two tall mahogany trees and sent it jouncing and fighting every inch of the way. There was, as Tad had said, no semblance of a trail; but the jeep sturdily plowed its way between tall, creeper-covered trees and over low underbrush. They had both been dripping wet even before they had left the village. Now they were as soaked as though they had been swimming.

Ann pushed her streaming hair from her eyes and dodged a creeper that swayed and swung in the wind. Tad was concentrating on negotiating the way through the jungle-like growth, thankful that up here it was not nearly as dense as it would have been on the lower level of the Cay.

They came out at last on the lip of the ravine and sat for a dazed moment in the threatening twilight, looking down the ravine. There was an opening where the sea washed in. Down there, in what must have been Mam'

Cleo's camp, the water was already well up above the six-foot level. There was no sign of a living creature.

"We're too late," said Ann huskily.

"The first big wave probably got her," Tad agreed.

And then in the fading light Ann saw something that looked like a bundle of old clothes plastered to the face of the ravine across from them. And above the bundle of old clothes was a dark face whose eyes rolled and whose hands clung with frantic strength to the low-growing bush that jutted out from the rocky side of the ravine.

"Tad!" she cried out. "There she is, over there on the other side. And she's alive."

She was out of the jeep and running along the edge of the ravine, even as Tad followed her, crying out:

"Ann! Come back here, you little fool. You can't get over there."

Ann did not even look back as she slipped over the lip of the ravine and began making her perilous way down its rough sides. Tad followed. But by the time he reached the water, Ann had already plunged in and was swimming against the waves, resting now and then to let them lift her up, until she finally was flung against the cliff which the old woman clung, gibbering in terror, watching them with eyes so big and so white that they seemed to swallow her wrinkled old ebony-hued face.

Ann and Tad managed the climb together. But when they reached the old woman she was too terrified to let go her hold on the bush that had been supporting her.

Ann spoke to her soothingly until at last she managed to break that frantic grip. When the old woman released the bush she slid into Ann's arms, a helpless weight, and only Tad's hand shooting out to grasp them, kept all three from tumbling headlong into the raging waters.

Clinging with one hand, Tad managed to steady Ann and the old woman enough to enable Ann to get one strong young arm firmly about the scrawny old body. And then between them they managed to get her down. When a wave reached up and caught them, they were grateful for the force with which it took them. For a long moment, supporting the old woman between them, they rested on the wave; then as it tried to hurl them to destruction, they began fighting against it, striving desperately to reach safety and the jeep above the lip of the ravine.

It seemed to both Ann and Tad that a century elapsed before at last they could pull themselves from the grip of the water and lie, panting and fighting for breath, before making the climb up to where the jeep waited.

The old woman sprawled between them lifelessly. When Ann had regained her breath, she touched the sodden body and said faintly, "She's alive, but only just. We've got to get some dry clothes on her and get her warm."

"Right," said Tad briefly, and swung the old woman across his shoulders, steadying her with one hand while he used the other to pull himself up the side of the ravine; followed by Ann.

When, after what seemed like years and years of the struggle, they crawled out on top of the ravine and the old woman lay sprawled between them, Tad looked back at the view below them and shuddered.

"And that," he told Ann breathlessly, "will be about as narrow an escape as either of us can ever hope to know."

Ann was examining the old woman, forgetful of the peril from which she and Tad had just emerged. She said anxiously, "We are nearer the mill than the hacienda or the clinic, so we'd better take her to the mill."

"Besides which," said Tad grimly, "the clinic is probably three feet under water by now, and the storm's not more than half over."

Together they lifted the old woman into the back of the jeep. Ann slid in beside her to steady her as Tad backed the jeep cautiously toward the road. Now that the immediate peril was over they were both aware of the foul, fetid odor of the old woman. Ann said faintly, "I can't help feeling what she needs most is a good hot bath with lots of soap. What an odor!"

"Well, she's had a good salt-water bath, that's for sure," Tad answered over his shoulder, and came out at last on the trail to the mill.

When they reached the mill everything was in darkness save for the flickering of candles and oil lamps. The island's privately owned power plant that operated the mill and the electrical equipment of the whole Cay had gone down in the storm.

There were sounds of voices and keening wails, and as the jeep came to a halt, people peered out of the wide-open doors through which the ox-carts were accustomed to drive.

"Hi," called Tad. "Somebody come here and help. We found Mam' Cleo, but she's in a bad way."

Nobody made a move to help. Instead, the refugees backed away from the door into the mill. A stout, middle-aged white man, his partly bald head fringed with red hair that matched his busy red whiskers, came striding out into the storm.

"Mam' Cleo, huh?" he said grimly. "That's all we need now—a *mama-loi* inside the mill—with these fool natives skittering and scattering like wild things."

He caught up the sodden body and strode back into the mill, with Ann and Tad following him. The native people all drew back away from the unconscious woman and eyed Ann and Tad with wide, scared eyes.

Ann glared around the crowded room and spoke sharply.

"You've all run to her when you were in trouble, and she's helped you. Now she's in trouble, and you're all shying away from her as if you were afraid of her. Somebody get me some blankets and dry clothes. Mr. Mac, what about a shot of our best rum? I imagine that's the only medicine we have here?"

"We've a first-aid kit, Miss Ann. Not much else we ever need here," answered McGuire, the engineer. "Here it is."

Ann stripped off the woman's wet clothes and scrubbed the skinny, frail old body hard with a rough towel, while the men stayed outside the room. When she had finished scrubbing she saw an old pouch on a dirty leather string about the old woman's scrawny neck and reached to remove it. But an instant of returning consciousness, perhaps a presentiment of danger, made the old woman put up a claw-like, dirty hand and clutch the bag with desperate strength.

Ann drew a deep hard breath, patted the dirty old hand and made no further attempt to remove what she knew to be Mam' Cleo's most cherished possession—her "conjure bag."

There were deep scratches and a gash or two on the old legs, and Ann cleansed these and bandaged the cuts. She rolled the old woman in warm blankets and stood erect, realizing for the first time how desperately tired she was. Water poured from her body, clad only in a sunsuit; her hair streamed about her face and water poured from it. But at the moment she wasn't conscious of anything except the aching weariness that seemed to reach to her very bones.

She clung to the edge of a heavy chair, and her eyes closed as she fought off the threat of unconsciousness. And then arms closed about her and lifted her as though she had been a child, and she looked with dazed eyes into Tad's face.

"Are you trying to catch pneumonia?" he demanded as though he were very angry with her. "Come on in my office and get some dry clothes on and warm yourself."

"I can't leave my patient," Ann stammered feebly.

"Can't leave your patient!" Tad snorted as he lifted her and carried her out of the room. "You risked your life to get her down from that ledge; you want to go on risking it just to stand and watch her sleep? You'll be a lot of good to her or everybody else if you're flat on your back fighting pneumonia, won't you?"

He plunked her down in his office and indicated a pile of clothes on a chair.

"Best I could do," he told her. "But at least they are dry and fresh out of the laundry. Now hurry into them while I get some coffee."

He went out and shut the door behind him.

Chapter Twelve

Tad knocked at the door just as Ann was drawing on the shirt that he had left for her. The pants were miles too big for her, but she had bundled them around her waist and tied them with a cord. The shirt was equally big, and she was rolling up the sleeves when Tad came in with a tray on which was a big blue and white enameled coffee-pot and some thick, man-sized sandwiches.

He eyed her as though startled by the khaki pants, rolled up to the knees; the soft white shirt with the tails hanging out over the thick bunch of the waist line; the sleeves rolled above her elbows; and her tumbled hair that she had tried to scrub dry. He chuckled as he put the tray down on his desk.

"Darling, you were never lovelier," he mocked her, and they both laughed in sheer relief from the tension that had gripped them for so long.

Ann revolved slowly before him in a model's airy stance and tilted her head as she glanced down at herself.

"I know a divine little dressmaker who simply must copy this confection for me," she drawled affectedly. "I'll be a sensation at the next Hanson concert."

Tad was pouring coffee for her, offering her a sandwich.

"Looks as if the storm might be letting up a bit," he said as they dropped wearily into chairs. "Or it could just be that the 'eye' of the storm is approaching."

"I should go and check on my patient," said Ann reluctantly.

"She's sleeping the sleep of the just," Tad told her. At her startled look he added hastily, "Oh, no, she's not dead. She's just asleep and snoring!"

Ann relaxed and drank deeply of her coffee.

"No one else needs medical attention?" she asked anxiously.

"Nobody," Tad told her, and grinned wryly. "Now that I've seen you in action, I suppose Clarita was wise in deciding you had to be a nurse. But heck, Ann, I'm sure going to miss you these next two years."

Ann nodded soberly. "And I'm going to miss you and the Cay and everybody," she admitted. "But do you know something, Tad? I'm going to miss you most of all. That's odd, isn't it?"

Tad said cautiously, "Fantastic. I wonder why that should be?"

Ann was chewing away hungrily at her sandwich, her eyes thoughtful. She spoke slowly, as though sorting out her thoughts, bringing them out into the open so she could study them.

Tad watched her and waited. Her tumbled, still damp chestnut-colored curls framed her small, intent face. There were smudges of weariness beneath her golden-brown eyes, and her face was, of course, entirely guiltless of makeup. Yet to Tad she was lovelier than she had ever been before; so lovely that he was secretly startled to realize his sudden awareness of that.

"I don't quite know, Tad," she said at last and looked up at him, a small frown drawing her brows together. "It's as if I'd only just met you. I mean it's as if all of a sudden you weren't just Tad, the bratty little boy I grew up with; but somebody strange and new and exciting. Why do you suppose that is?"

"I don't know," said Tad carefully. "But I was not a bratty little boy. I resent the allegation!"

"I thought you were."

"Want to know what I thought of you when we were busy growing up?"

"Thanks, no," said Ann hastily. "I'd much rather not. I'm just sort of curious to know what you think of me now. All of a sudden that's terribly important."

Tad put his coffee cup down and leaned against the desk, his hands folded tightly together, his eyes intent on her and carrying a veiled message that she could not quite understand.

"What do I think of you now?" he repeated slowly, carefully. "Why, I think you're a pretty wonderful person, and David Lochran will be just about the luckiest guy in the world if he comes back here as your husband."

"Oh, but he won't," Ann cut in swiftly. "I haven't had a chance to tell you. He is going to marry Julia, and they are going to work together. They haven't decided just where yet, but I'm quite sure it won't be at the Cay. That's why I have to go back to Blalock for two more years: so the Cay can have medical care."

Tad was startled and his eyes narrowed slightly.

"So you've lost David," he said gently.

Ann said quickly, "You can't lose what you've never had, Tad." She added quietly, "I don't think I really mind a single bit. And that's funny, isn't it?"

"Hilarious," said Tad, and went on waiting.

"You don't really mind, do you, Tad?"

"Mind what?"

"Well, that Julia's in love with David."

"Now why, in the name of all that's sane, sound and reasonable, should I mind that?"

"Well, Julia's a wonderful girl, and she's somebody you haven't known all your life, and I thought just maybe you might like her a lot."

"I do, of course."

"But not love? I mean you're not in love with Julia?"

For a moment he was quite still, and then he said slowly, evenly and with utter conviction, as though he wanted the simple words to impress themselves deeply on her consciousness, "I'm not in love with Julia. I have never been in love with Julia. Nor do I have the faintest intention of ever being in love with Julia."

Ann beamed radiantly at him, her smile removing momentarily the deep, aching weariness on her face.

"Oh, Tad, I'm so glad!" she breathed joyously. "I mean, I would have felt terrible if I'd brought her here and you'd fallen in love with her and then she'd gone away."

"Leaving me to eat out my heart because of unrequited love?" Tad mocked.

Ann flushed. "Well, I've heard it's not a very comfortable process."

"I wouldn't know."

"I hope you never will, Tad."

There was a silence in which they looked away from each other as though each were fearful of what the other might see in his eyes.

"I'm sorry about Lochran," Tad said at last.

"Sorry?"

"That the Cay isn't going to have him as a resident doctor," Tad told her. "But I'm most sorry of all that you'll be away for two long years."

"It's a terribly long time, isn't it?" Ann agreed mournfully.

"Terribly."

"I'll get another vacation a year from now."

"Well, I suppose that's something to look forward to," Tad told her.

Ann's carefully maintained composure broke and she stammered, "Oh, Tad, Tad, I don't want to go! I don't want to!"

Tad's arms reached down and drew her up to him and held her closely. His voice, low and soothing, murmured endearments and offered a comfort that even in that moment he knew held no solace.

For a long moment she clung to him, sobbing; and then she drew a little away from him and stared up at him, her eyes wide with a sudden realization, her tear-wet face flushed.

"Why, Tad!" she breathed, her voice touched with wonder. "Are we in love with each other?"

Tad grinned at her ardently. "Well, of course I can speak only for myself. But speaking for myself, honey, I'm plumb stomp-down crazy about you. I've been falling in love with you for years, but it took a hurricane to make me realize it!"

"Oh, Tad!" she breathed, and came once more into his arms and clung to him for an exquisite, wordless moment while her kiss met, accepted and fulfilled his own.

After a time—neither had the faintest idea how long it had been—she drew away from him and looked up at him sorrowfully.

"Oh, Tad, darling, darling Tad," she mourned. "How can I *possibly* go away and leave you for two whole years?"

"That's easy," said Tad masterfully. "You're not going to."

Startled, she protested, "But Clarita wants me to. She'll be heartbroken if I don't complete my training."

"She'll be hurt, of course." Tad was willing to concede that much. "She'll be disappointed. But you and I between us will manage to find somewhere a doctor who will come here when Dr. John has to give up. I don't know where or how, but we'll find somebody. And you're staying right here, and you're going to marry me."

She was staring up at him, wide-eyed.

"How does that sound?" he asked when she didn't seem to be able to find a voice with which to answer.

"It sounds too good to be true," she breathed at last.

"It's too good not to be true," Tad corrected her, and grinned. "To think that all these years Clarita and Mom have been hoping you and I would fall in love and marry, and neither of us had the slightest idea of doing it. What do you suppose made us change our minds?"

Ann laughed joyously. "Maybe we're just contrary."
"Could be!" Tad grinned at her. "You were always a stubborn little critter."
"And so were you! You were a bratty small boy!" she countered.
"And you were a bratty little girl!" Tad pointed out. "Maybe we deserve each other. Maybe nobody else could get along with us."
"Then isn't it wonderful nobody else has to?" Ann laughed.
For a long moment they were silent, looking deep into each other's eyes and seeing there what each wanted most to see.
Clarita would be disappointed, they knew, that Ann was not going to complete her nurse's training. But they were both so sure of Clarita's love for them that they knew she would not deny them their happiness. Somewhere, somehow, they would find a doctor for the Cay. But for the present it was enough just to rejoice in their newly discovered love and the happiness of that discovery. . . .
Toward morning the storm ebbed. The wind slowed and the rain ceased its hard, thrumming pounding. By the break of dawn the storm had passed on and the sun rose.
Ann and Tad stood in front of the main building of the mill and looked with wide eyes at the devastation the storm had left in its wake and on which now the newly risen sun was shining benevolently. There was the sound of rushing waters, and the trail down the hillside was strewn with debris. Here and there tall trees had been uprooted and lay across the trail. But overhead there was a blue sky with only a scudding white puffball of a cloud moving before the fresh trade wind.
The workers were already clearing the trail, anxious to get back to the village and find out what had happened to friends and relatives left there.
"We'd better take Mam' Cleo to the clinic," Ann suggested worriedly. "Everybody else seems to be in good shape and able to get down by foot or by oxcart. But Mam' Cleo is still unconscious. I can hold her in the back of the jeep, and you can drive. Don't you think we'd better get started?"
"Dr. John's going to love you for bringing her in to

him," Tad said ruefully. "He doesn't have much affection for witch doctors."

"I know," Ann answered uneasily. "But we can't just let her die, darling. And she may if she isn't given skilled attention. I just don't have the training to diagnose her case and decide what's best for her. And even if I did, we don't have the medicine she probably needs. Oh, Tad, dearest, we've just got to get her to the clinic."

"Sure, honey, sure," said Tad comfortingly. "It'll be a rough trip for you and for her, too. But we'll do our best. Let's get started."

They went back into the mill and to the vast room where Mam' Cleo lay on an improvised bed. She moaned and stirred restlessly and lapsed once more into unconsciousness, and Tad bent to gather her up in his arms. One of the native women came swiftly forward with a protesting gesture.

"You take her away, Boss?" she asked.

"Down to the clinic, Bessie, so that Dr. John can look after her," Ann answered before Tad could speak.

"No, no, no, *Señorita!* No, *Señor* Boss. You must not take her there," protested the woman, and hovered protectingly above the old woman, her eyes deeply troubled. "Mam' Cleo a doctor her own self. She be all right. You cannot take her away."

Tad straightened and eyed the group that had drawn closer to the frail creature on the improvised bed. He looked from one dark, anxious face to another, and the frown deepened between his brows.

"Look here," he pointed out sharply. "She's got to have medical attention, skilled medical attention. Miss Ann hasn't the training or the medicine—"

"Mam' Cleo have medicine," the woman he had called Bessie insisted, and touched with shrinking fingers the filthy old pouch hung about the scrawny neck on its worn leather thing. "You and *Señorita* go away. Mam' Cleo be all right. You no take her."

They spoke in the native patois that was an odd, slurring mixture of French, Spanish and a sort of hodgepodge of their own. But to Tad and Ann it was a language as familiar as their own English, and though Ann had been away for a year she found it easy both to follow and to speak.

She tried gently to explain to Bessie and to the others what she and Tad planned to do. But the dark faces of the group grew ever more mutinous. At last Tad straightened, turned to Ann and said quietly, "We don't want to start a ruckus, and it looks as if we would if we insisted on moving her down to the clinic."

Ann looked about the group and then back to Tad.

"Then we'll go down, and I'll describe her condition to Dr. John and David, and they'll tell me what to do for her and then we can come back," she yielded. "After all, that might be the wisest thing to do. I don't know whether she would be able to stand the trip, anyway."

Tad turned back to the group and addressed them in patois.

"We'll leave her here then," he told them. "But I shall expect you to look after her very carefully. Miss Ann and I will be back as soon as we can and bring what Dr. John says is the proper medicine for her. Do you understand?"

The entire group nodded its understanding, and Tad and Ann hurried out. As they moved toward the jeep, parked just inside the open doorway of the big double entrance, McGuire came toward them, wiping his oily hands on a piece of filthy waste.

"You're leaving?" he asked, and went on briskly, "Tell 'em at the hacienda we hope to have the power plant going within a few hours; in any case before dark. They can count on electric lights by the time they are needed."

"That'll be good news," Tad said. "We wanted to take Mam' Cleo to the clinic where Dr. John could look after her. But it looked as if there would be a riot if we attempted it. So we'll be back with whatever Dr. John thinks may be the most effective medicine for her."

McGuire grinned mirthlessly.

"The most effective medicine for that old witch would have been to leave her right where you found her," he said grimly. "The Cay would be a much healthier and more decent place without her."

"Well, maybe so, but we couldn't let her drown," Tad answered.

"No, I suppose not," McGuire answered heavily, and turned back to his job.

Ann and Tad climbed into the jeep and started the slow, torturous journey down the trail that was being cleared by the workmen, who stood aside to let the jeep pass, throwing up weary hands in greeting as it rolled past.

When the jeep reached the junction of the trail that led to the hacienda and the village lay in view, Tad brought the jeep to a halt so sharp that he and Ann were flung forward against the instrument panel. Both stared with wide, horror-stricken eyes at the scene below them.

Once there had been a village there: a neat row of white cottages, palm-thatched, facing each other across a wide sandy road. Now there was only water, dirty, foam-flecked, debris-strewn. Here and there a chicken coop floated; the palm thatch of a roof slid aimlessly; tall palms lay on the water, their tops swirling in the booming waves that rushed in.

"It's gone!" Ann said at last when she could break the paralysis of shock that gripped her. "The whole village is gone!"

"That must have been a brute of a tidal wave!" Tad told her, and spoke softly as though awed by the magnitude of the disaster.

"There have been hurricanes before that struck at the Cay and high tides that have risen in the street a foot or two," Ann murmured, "but never anything like this. Tad, it's horrible! It scares me!"

"Me, too," Tad answered honestly. "Thank heaven we were able to evacuate the villagers before it happened."

Ann said fearfully, "The clinic, Tad? Is that gone, too?"

"We'll have to see," Tad answered, and cautiously slid the jeep into the trail that led to where the village had been, but was no longer.

They both gave little cries of relief when they saw the square, solidly built white clinic building and the water lapping at the drive. Dr. John had insisted on having the clinic built this far from the village and on a rise of the mountain crowned by the hacienda. Now they could understand his far-seeing wisdom.

Tad drove through a foot or two of water in the drive and felt the jeep plunge into washed-out places. As they came within reach of the steps and he stopped the jeep, they saw with a lift of their hearts that the watermark on the bottom step had receded, and knew it meant that the flood was easing.

Ann ran ahead up the steps and into the building, and Tad followed her. Inside the small lobby a group of dark-skinned people huddled together, and there were small, terrified cries as Ann and Tad came in.

Tad spoke to them soothingly as Ann hurried on into the small ward with its six beds and its treatment table. Dr. John sat at the treatment table, a cup of coffee held in his shaking hand. Each of the beds was occupied, and Julia stood beside one, her fingers on a thin wrist in which she was counting the pulse.

Dr. John looked up as Ann came swiftly into the room, and his tired eyes widened as he took in her garb: Tad's pants rolled halfway to her knees and the over-sized shirt.

"Well, well, it's Little Orphan Annie." He grinned at her. "And where have you been this night, chick? And what a devil of a night it's been."

Julia put down the thin wrist, tucked a cover gently above the occupant of the bed and turned to face them. Her own garb was quite as unconventional as Ann's: a pair of once-white duck pants, undoubtedly out of Dr. John's own wardrobe, and a sheet wrapped around her, pinned at the neck and tied at the waist, leaving her arms bare.

She managed a faint smile at Ann and said, "I wonder what Miss Marshall would say if she could see us now? Not much like Blalock's o.r., is it?"

David, hearing their voices, came in from Dr. John's tiny office and stood looking at them. And though his face was gray with fatigue, he managed a faint smile.

"I must say we are a rough-looking crew, but everything is under control, for which let us all give humble and devout thanks," he greeted them. "How are things at the mill, Tad?"

"Under control," said Tad. "McGuire said that the power would be back on by tonight and we could count on electric lights by the time they are needed."

"That's good news!" said David, and exchanged warm smiles with Julia. "At least we won't have to do an emergency appendectomy by candlelight again."

Ann said quickly, "Dr. John, Mam' Cleo's up at the

mill, and I think she's got pneumonia. But I didn't dare try to treat her, even if I'd had anything to treat her with. So I came down to ask you what to do for her and to get some medicine for her."

Dr. John said sharply, "So you found the old witch, did you? That's too bad!"

"Now you hush!" snapped Ann hotly. "Tad and I risked our lives to rescue her, and now everybody wishes we'd let her drown. She's a pitiful old woman and she needs help, and I demand that something be done for her."

Dr. John's bushy eyebrows went up, and he stared at the girl as though he had never seen her before.

"You demand that something be done for the old witch doctor?" repeated Dr. John as though not quite sure he had heard her correctly. "Why, you young snippet, you mind your manners."

"And you remember your Hippocratic oath, Dr. John," snapped Ann. "You pledged yourself to the care of the sick, the injured, the ailing. I don't know the oath by heart, but I bet there's something in it about having no regard for race, creed or color. If there isn't there ought to be!"

David, a twinkle in his eyes, said quickly, "There is, Ann. I can assure you there is. But Dr. John is in no shape to make that journey. I'll be happy to go along and see what I can do for the old girl. Tell me again what you think she needs."

Ann rapidly outlined the symptoms, and David listened intently, while Julia competently packed a black bag for David. When she had finished, Tad said mutinously, "Look, I've got to get Ann to the hacienda before she falls apart."

"Why not let me take Ann home?" suggested Julia. "I'd like some uniforms and a hot shower, and we need some food here for the patients and for their relatives in the lobby. Dr. John can take over until I get back."

"Can you drive a jeep?" asked Tad.

Julia managed a faintly impish smile.

"I've never tried, so I don't know," she admitted. "But I can surely make the effort and hope for the best."

"Then, Tad, you and David take your jeep and go back to the mill and Mam' Cleo," said Ann. "Julia and

I will run up to the hacienda and get some clothes and some food and come right back."

She turned courteously to Dr. John. "I believe that will be the best arrangement, don't you, Doctor?"

"I think it will, Nurse," said Dr. John as formally.

Ann sniffed disdainfully at the raillery in his eyes and his voice and turned to Julia.

"Then let's get going," she said briskly. For a moment her eyes met Tad's and clung, and it was as though she had kissed him.

David and Julia exchanged swift, startled glances, but Dr. John merely smiled as the four of them hurried out.

Chapter Thirteen

Tad and David drove off first. When they had reached the road, Ann and Julia followed them. The water was dropping slowly, but there was still a vast splash as the two jeeps hit the road. Then as they turned north along the trail that rose steeply, they were free of the water. Both jeeps had to travel with caution, however. At the junction of the two trails, David looked over his shoulder and lifted a hand in salute to Ann, who waved back at him. The next moment the two jeeps had gone their separate ways.

Negotiating the badly washed trail, mindful of trees torn down by the terrific winds. Ann scowled at the road ahead, then managed a glance at Julia.

"I'm awfully sorry that this happened while you and David were here," she said apologetically.

Julia ran her fingers through her disheveled hair and drew a deep, hard breath before she managed an answering smile.

"I'm not," she answered. "It's been a terrific experience. Oh, of course I'm terribly sorry about the village being washed away and all that. But of course you'll build it back, won't you?"

"Well, of course," Ann answered as though shocked by the question. "We'll build as fast as we can get the necessary supplies. It must have been pretty bad for you and David last night."

"Fortunately, most of the villagers had been evacuated, so we only caught a few that were unable to make the trip," Julia answered. "There were a couple of maternity cases—both boys—and the appendectomy. The rest was chiefly hysteria and the like. When the water began rising, it was a bit disturbing."

"Ha!" Ann scorned the word. "Disturbing my eye! Is that the way an R.N. considers a flood-tide and power failure and all the rest of it, to say nothing of hurricane winds and a deluge of rain?"

Despite her weariness, Julia smiled.

"Well, R.N.'s are taught they must maintain composure and move swiftly without running and a lot of other things," she admitted.

Ann eased the jeep over a hole in the road where the wind and rain had washed out a huge rock.

"Then I guess there's not much use my trying to be an R.N.," she admitted frankly. "I was scared pea-green yesterday when Tad and I were trying to pry that poor old scarecrow, Mam' Cleo, from the rock to bring her to safety."

"But the point is, Ann dear, you did it!" Julia pointed out.

"Well, sure, but that was because she was a part of the Cay and I couldn't leave her there. The water would have swamped her in another hour or less," Ann answered. "But I don't know if I could have done it anywhere but at the Cay."

She took her eyes from the trail for a moment, glanced at Julia and confessed humbly, "Julia, I don't want to be an R.N."

"Don't you, dear?" Julia's tone was gentle. "You'd make a good one."

"Maybe." Ann was unconvinced. "I just want to stay here on the Cay and marry Tad and be idiotically happy!"

Julia hesitated, and then she asked, "But, dear, hasn't all that we've gone through convinced you how badly the Cay needs a skilled medical attendant? Dr. John won't last forever, you know."

Ann nodded, her young mouth bitter. "And he's terribly old-fashioned and hasn't kept up with modern medical miracles and the new drugs and all. Sure, I know that. But, Julia, I don't want to leave the Cay ever again!"

"Don't you, dear?" Julia's eyes were warmly compassionate. "I can understand that. I think if I were in your place, nothing could lure me away."

Ann asked eagerly, "You like the Cay, Julia?"

"I love it!"

"Even the way it looks now?"

"Even the way it looks now!"

"I'm so glad!"

The hacienda was ahead of them now. Up here, aside from a few trees that had been felled and the wreck of the blossoms on the shrubbery, there were not too many signs of the hurricane.

As the jeep slid to a halt, Mary came running out to them. As she saw Julia beside Ann, instead of Tad as she had hoped, her face altered slightly. As the two girls got out of the jeep, Mary's brows went up and her eyes widened.

"Good heavens, you look like a pair of tramps!" she gasped. "Where have you been?"

Ann moved stiffly, flexing muscles she hadn't realized until now were stiffening, and answered, "I've been at the mill and Julia's been at the clinic, and all we want at the moment is a good hot shower and some clean clothes and food. I seem to remember vaguely that I had a sandwich in the not too distant past and a cup of what passed for coffee at what was called breakfast, but it's only a vague memory."

Mary drew them into the house, and Clarita, no longer making the painful effort to walk but quite content to remain in her wheel-chair, propelled it toward them, calling out to Ann as she came.

Ann knelt swiftly and cradled her close and said as though to a frightened child, "There, there, darling. Everything's just fine and dandy."

Mary hurried Julia off to take a hot shower and change into a fresh uniform, leaving Ann and Clarita alone.

"I hate to tell you, darling," said Ann when the first transports of their greeting were over, "but the village is gone."

"I know," said Clarita as though it were of no importance. "Mary and I saw it happen from the terrace out there. We thanked God that all the people were out and that only the livestock suffered. We'll build back, dear, and restock. But tell me about yourself. Where were you?"

Swiftly Ann told her of the rescue of Mam' Cleo and of the journey she and Tad had made with the old woman back to the mill. Clarita listened and looked aghast at the realization of the risk Ann had taken, apparently without even realizing it, because she had been so concerned for the safety of Mam' Cleo. Her arms tightened about the girl as Ann finished, and then she drew a deep, hard breath.

"I'm very proud of you, darling," she said huskily. "And now you must go and change. I've never seen such a grotesque outfit."

Ann stood up, revolved before Clarita and laughed at the look in the eyes that were turned to her.

"Tad gave them to me." Ann laughed. "They don't really do anything for me, do they?"

"Indeed they don't," Clarita answered. "But at that, they probably saved you from pneumonia. Run and soak in a good hot tub, darling, and then get into bed and sleep for the next twelve hours."

"Oh, I can't do that; sleep, I mean," Ann protested. "I'll change and then I'll have some breakfast, lots and lots of breakfast. And then I have to drive Julia back to the clinic. Maybe I can help out there. Dr. John's pretty beat up, and Julia and David must be, too."

She bent, brushed her lips against Clarita's cheek and went out of the room and up the stairs.

In her own room she found Mary just emerging from the bathroom, steamy and fragrant with bath salts lavishly poured into hot water.

"I'll see about some breakfast for you and Julia," said Mary. At the door she hesitated a moment and asked, "Is Tad all right?"

"Oh, Tad's fine!" Ann glowed as she stepped out of Tad's borrowed garments, her hands lingering caressingly upon them.

Mary's eyes widened slightly, but she went out of the room and closed the door gently behind her without speaking.

After her steaming, fragrant bath Ann dressed herself in one of the first year student nurse uniforms she had brought home with her, perched her cherished cap airily on her head and went down the stairs.

Julia was already at the table, crisp and immaculate in her white uniform and her cap. As Ann came in she looked up, smiled warmly and said, "Well, hi, there, Firstie!"

Ann laughed and sat down as Mary brought a well-laden tray from the kitchen. Clarita, in her chair at the head of the table, accepted a cup of coffee and watched as the two girls plunged hungrily into their food.

"Poor David! Poor Dr. John! Poor Tad!" said Julia, happily absorbing delicately golden scrambled eggs and a thick slice of ham.

"Never mind. We'll cook them a feast when we get back to the clinic," Ann told her. "Did you pack a basket of food for us to take, Mary?"

"Of course, dear. Julia said you had six patients and their anxious relatives. I'm sure there will be enough for all of them, and for the staff as well!"

"The staff!" said Ann, round-eyed. "Julia, that's *us!*"

Julia laughed. "So it is, chick. And one of these days you'll be a part of the staff of Blalock Memorial!"

Ann nodded soberly.

Clarita said, "Your uniform is very becoming, Ann."

Ann looked down at it, and her mouth curled in a faintly cynical smile. "It should be. It cost enough."

"Why, was it so very expensive?" asked Clarita wonderingly.

"Oh, not in money," Ann answered; "just in hard work and unpleasant tasks and the privation of a year away from the Cay."

Julia looked swiftly about the table and stood up.

"No thanks, Mrs. Delehenty, no more coffee," she said briskly. "We'd better get going, Ann. Dr. John and David will be needing us."

"Sure," said Ann obediently, and rose.

"But you two girls are so tired. You should go to bed and get some sleep," protested Clarita.

"We'll send David and Dr. John up for a nap and a hot bath as soon as we get back," answered Julia. "And if you could get Dr. John to sleep a twelve-hour stretch it would do him a tremendous amount of good. He's just about worn out."

"We'll try," Clarita answered ruefully. "But he's pretty determined and devoted to his duty."

"David is fascinated by some of Dr. John's research and admires him tremendously," Julia said.

"There's only one Dr. John," Mary answered, and walked with them to the door.

When the jeep had gone, Mary came back to the dining room where Clarita still sat at the head of the table, her coffee cold in its cup, her eyes on space.

"More coffee, darling? Mary asked.

Clarita seemed not to hear her. Looking up, she met Mary's eyes.

"Was I a brute, Mary?" Clarita asked huskily.

"What an idiotic question, darling," Mary answered swiftly. "You couldn't do a cruel, callous thing if you took lessons for the rest of your life."

"She was very unhappy at the hospital," Clarita said.

Mary hesitated and then answered gently, "I suppose so, Clarita. But we both know it had to be. She knows, too, now."

For a moment both women were silent, and then Clarita asked, "What are you thinking, Mary?"

Mary answered honestly, "The same thing you are thinking, darling."

The two women smiled at each other, and neither spoke again.

Ann and Julia were overjoyed to discover, when they reached the clinic, that the water in the drive was dropping, although they could see huge waves still breaking over what had once been the village.

Inside they found David and Dr. John bending above a cot on which lay Mam' Cleo. Ann gasped, "Oh, did they let you bring her away?"

David looked at her, a startled frown between his brows.

"But of course I brought her away," he said. "I couldn't leave her there, could I? She needs careful nursing. One lung is completely filled, and her fever is high. She's really an amazing old woman. I don't suppose anybody has any idea of her age?"

"I don't," Ann answered. "She's always been here, according to the natives. She was an old woman when I was born."

"Well, it's amazing how she could go through what she has endured and still be around," David admitted.

"Will she live?" asked Ann.

Once more David gave her a surprised, disapproving glance.

"She's alive at the moment, and while there's life—"

"Oh, she'll live," Dr. John cut him off. "You can't kill her kind. A living personification of evil is practically indestructible."

David and Julia exchanged swift glances, and Ann said briskly to Dr. John, "You're needed at the hacienda, Dr. John."

Dr. John eyed her coldly.

"Trying to get rid of me?" he demanded.

"As a matter of fact, I am," Ann answered. "With David and Julia and me here, you're needed much worse at the hacienda. You *do* remember that we took the sick and infirm from the village there, don't you? Do you expect Clarita and Mary to look after them while you sit here and hurl insults at a sick old woman who can't defend herself? Hop to it, Dr. John. Come on; I'll drive you."

She glanced at David and Julia, and raised her eyebrows in a question that David answered with a slight nod.

"Yes, run along, Ann. Dr. John is too tired to drive, I know. That's a brutal drive for a tired man," Julia began.

"Well, what about a young girl who's been running around like a chicken with its head chopped off for the last thirty-six hours or more?" demanded Dr. John. "And she's made the round trip once."

Ann laid a firm hand on his arm and steered him toward the door.

"I never get worried about you, darling, until you get nasty," she told him coolly but very firmly. "And you've been nasty-mouthing everybody in reach of your voice now for hours. So pick up your feet, pal, and let's get going somewhere where you're needed."

Dr. John shot David an inimical glance.

"As, of course, I'm not here," he growled.

"As, of course, you aren't here," Ann assured him firmly, and over his shoulder winked merrily at Julia, who winked back at her.

As the sound of the jeep died away down the drive, Julia looked up at David and gave him a faint smile.

"Would you like some breakfast?" she suggested.

David lifted his eyes from the patient in front of him and seemed to come back from a long distance.

"Breakfast? Oh, yes, I don't believe I've had breakfast, have I?" He seemed surprised.

"You haven't, and only a makeshift supper. I'll get it ready for you and then feed the patients," Julia told him.

Later, when their morning duties had been attended to, they stood side by side on the steps, inhaling the fresh, salt-laden air and watching the ruined village below them. David drew a deep breath and glanced down at Julia.

"I'm beginning to understand why the Cay means so much to Ann," he said slowly. "It's an oasis of peace and quiet in the hurly-burly of the outside world."

"Peace and quiet?" Julia fairly hooted at him, and threw out a hand that indicated the destruction the storm had created. "If what's happened in the last twenty-four to thirty-six hours is your idea of peace and quiet—"

David laughed, lit a cigarette for her and one for himself and answered, "Oh, well, back at Blalock we had emergencies, remember? And there are tornadoes and cyclones, and the States have had their share of hurricanes and tidal waves. I was thinking of the Cay the way it was when we first came; the way it will be again as soon as the place is rebuilt."

"It *was* lovely," Julia admitted.

"Some of Dr. John's research is terrifically interesting," David said slowly, deeply thoughtful. "A pity he probably won't live to complete it."

Julia waited, and after a moment he looked down at her, frowning slightly.

"I suppose you'd think I was a double-barreled, brass-bound, copper-rivited idiot if I told you I'd like to stay here and complete his work?" he asked, with more than a trace of uneasiness in his voice.

Julia looked away from him and steadied her voice with such an effort that her words sounded cold and judicial, "You'd have to be very sure that was what you really want to do, David; very sure that it is a post for an ambitious young doctor who wants to get ahead in his profession."

A shadow touched David's tired face.

"Well, yes, I suppose so," he agreed reluctantly. "But wouldn't it be worth-while to help Dr. John? The results of his research could be of tremendous benefit not only to the Cay but to all the many places in the world where tropical diseases are a scourge."

"What about the work you planned with your friends back home?"

"The clinic we were planning to set up?" he asked. "That, of course, would be interesting, but not half as much as working here at the Cay with Dr. John and then carrying on for him when he is no longer able to work."

Julia was silent, still avoiding his eyes, and after a moment David said quietly, "There is only one thing I have to be sure about. I am already very sure that it's what *I* want. But I have to be sure about something else that is even more important than my own wishes."

"And that's?"

"That's whether or not you could be content to stay here."

For an instant she held her breath, and at last when she could be sure of her voice she said, "Of course. You'd need a nurse."

"I don't need a nurse," David protested violently. "I need a wife! I need you! I won't stay unless you're willing to stay with me."

Julia said evenly, "Oh, Ann will finish her training."

David caught her by the shoulders and swung her around so that she had to face him, and scowled ferociously at her.

"Blast it, I'm trying to tell you that I love you and want you to marry me, and if you will, I'll go anywhere in the world that you want to go!"

Julia laughed and slid into his arms, her own about him.

"Well, for Peter Rabbit's sake, why didn't you say so without all this foolin' around?" she demanded.

Startled, David asked dazedly, "Does that mean that you will?"

"Well, of course it does, you blessed dope!" she told him. "I've been in love with you for ages. And if you didn't know it, then you're just about the only member of the personnel at Blalock Memorial that didn't."

"Well, I'll be darned!" said David so softly she could scarcely believe she had really heard the words.

Puzzled, she asked, "You didn't suspect that I was in love with you?"

"How could I? You were always so matter of fact, so impersonal. And anyway I didn't think I was worthy of you—" David realized the words were trite and grinned apologetically at her. "In about a minute, I'll be dropping one one knee in front of you, with my hand on my heart, bleating, 'Miss Anderson, Miss Julia—may I call you Julia?—will you do me the honor of marrying me?' "

"And I'll blush and flutter my eyelashes and simper, "Oh, Dr. Lochran, this is *so* sudden! But thanks, I'd love to!' "

David studied her for a moment.

"Well, what do you know?" he marveled softly.

And then he kissed her.

Chapter Fourteen

It was a few days later that Ann, at the dinner table, said lightly, "Miss Marshall's going to be pretty mad at me when I get back. I'll be late returning from my vacation."

She glanced across the table at Tad, who gave her a tender look that brought deep color to her cheeks.

"Well, she surely couldn't expect you to return through a hurricane," Clarita protested. "It's just now getting safe for a boat to leave the Cay and take you to Aux Cayes and on to Port-au-Prince to catch a plane."

"Oh, excuses make no difference to Miss Marshall," Ann insisted. "She'd expect me to swim back if there was no other way."

"Surely she can't be that rigid in her adherence to schedules," Clarita answered.

"Ha!" Ann scoffed. "Remember when she wouldn't let

Jessie off for even a week-end when her father was so badly hurt?"

"I remember," said Julia briefly.

Dr. John cocked his white head, his bushy brows arched.

"If you're trying to say Vada Marshall is a slave-driver—" he began loftily.

"Oh, she doesn't carry a bull-whip to lick the probationers into obedience, lambie," said Ann cheerfully. "She just gives you a look that would freeze an ice cube and tells you about rules and regulations and stuff."

"Well, rules and regulations are very important in a hospital," Dr. John insisted. "Do you find Vada so unpleasant, Julia?"

Julia laughed. "Oh, don't try to embroil me in this argument, Doctor, I'm strictly neutral. Remember, I'm no longer under Miss Marshall's authority."

"I suppose she is a strict disciplinarian," David joined in the conversation. "But she's a fine woman, and she has a tough job."

"Oh, well, leave us not argue," said Ann, and dismissed the subject.

After dinner, as the others were going into the big drawing room for coffee, Tad drew Ann back with him into the hall.

"You haven't told Clarita about us?" His tone was accusing.

"Darling, I just haven't been able to screw up my courage," she pleaded. "I know she's going to be terribly hurt, and I hate hurting her. But, Tad, I don't want to leave you and the Cay."

"Well, don't give that a thought," said Tad grimly. "You're not going to. We'll go in there right now and tell her."

"No, Tad, let me tell her when she and I are alone," begged Ann.

"And when do you plan to tell her?"

"Tonight," Ann promised. "I'll tell her tonight. I promise."

"And you don't want any help from me?"

"Well, gollies, why should I?" Ann was incensed. "I don't think there'll be any fighting. She won't hit me, and I won't hit her, so why would I need help?"

"Well, so be it then. But I'll be standing by in case you want me to back you up. I'll be on the terrace, and all you'll have to do is call me."

"I will, Tad. Only there really won't be any need," Ann assured him, speaking with more confidence than she really felt.

Tad looked down at her, and there was uneasiness in his eyes.

"Promise me, Ann, that you won't become sorry for her and give in?"

"I promise, Tad."

"She's going to be terribly disappointed, and you're such a softie and so crazy about her that—well, somehow I don't quite trust you not to give in."

"I won't, Tad. Truly I won't," she insisted earnestly.

"Because if you do, I'll refuse to take you to the mainland and you'll have to swim," Tad told her ominously.

"I'm a good swimmer, but not that good," she agreed, and gave him her lips and rested for a long moment in his arms.

It was some time later that Ann tapped lightly at the door of Clarita's room and Mary opened the door.

"Come in, dear," Clarita called. Mary smiled at Ann and went out.

Ann stood hesitant for a moment, and then she came to Clarita and knelt and put her arms about her, holding her close.

"What is it dear?" Clarita asked after a period in which the girl obviously struggled for words.

"I'm afraid you're going to be very disappointed, darling," Ann mumbled miserably.

"I suppose you want to tell me that you don't want to go back to the hospital to finish your training?" said Clarita.

Ann gasped and stared at Clarita, for the moment bereft of speech. Clarita smiled very tenderly.

"You want to stay here at the Cay and marry Tad, don't you, darling?" she asked.

Ann caught her breath and her eyes flew wide.

"How did you know?" she stammered.

"I'm not quite blind, honey," Clarita told her. "I've been a little hurt that you didn't come to me as soon as you and Tad made up your minds."

"You don't mind?" Ann asked. "You're not disappointed?"

"You foolish child!" Clarita told her. "It's something I have hoped would happen: that you would find each other and realize that what you feel for each other is not merely the affection of a brother and sister."

"Oh, it's certainly not that." Ann replied quickly.

"I'm glad," said Clarita. "He's a fine boy, and I know you will be very happy with him."

"But, Clarita, what about a doctor for the Cay? We need one so badly."

"We've got one," said Clarita, and smiled. "David and Julia are getting married and staying on permanently at the Cay."

The announcement bowled Ann over, and for a long moment she could only sit there staring at Clarita, her mouth agape.

"They are?" she managed at last.

Clarita nodded. "So you see there is no longer any necessity of your finishing your training," she said. "You and Tad will help rebuild the Cay, and David and Julia will complete Dr. John's work, and the four of you will, I know, live happily ever after."

"Tad and I will," Ann answered radiantly. "And I do hope David and Julia will. Do you think they will, Clarita? They won't get bored and leave all of a sudden?"

"I don't think there's any possibility of that, dear," Clarita answered, and there was a spark of merriment in her eyes. "And even if they should, I promise not to bundle you up and send you back to Blalock."

Ann laughed. "Oh, Tad wouldn't allow that," she answered.

Clarita's brows went up a little. "Oh, he wouldn't! Where is he, by the way? I'd like to give him my blessing, as well as you."

"Oh, he's out on the terrace," Ann answered, "in case I need help."

Honestly puzzled, Clarita asked, "What kind of help could you need?"

"Oh, he was afraid maybe you'd be so disappointed about my not going back to Blalock that he'd have to help me persuade you that my place was rightfully here at the Cay."

Clarita nodded. "Well, bring him in. I'd like to convince him that the one thing I've ever wanted for you was your happiness, and that I sent you away with the very kindly intent of giving you both a chance to find out that you really loved each other."

Ann stared at her, round-eyed. "Was that really the reason, Clarita?"

Clarita gave a small, friendly chuckle. "Oh, well, there was the very good chance that you might like being a nurse and finish your training, even before you realized you were in love with him."

"But how could you possibly know that, Clarita, when I didn't even suspect it myself?" Ann wondered.

"I'm much older, dear, and I hope I'm wiser than you about such things," Clarita answered gently. "You'd been here together all your lives, and you'd become so accustomed to each other it seemed to me that if you were separated for a while you might suddenly realize that you were very important to each other."

Ann stared at her. "Then you didn't really care whether I became an R.N. or not, just as long as I discovered I was in love with Tad?"

"Of course I did, dear," Clarita corrected her. "And if David and Julia hadn't come home with you and decided they wanted to stay, I'm afraid I might have insisted that you go back and get your degree."

"Even if I'd found out I didn't want to go because I was in love with Tad?" asked Ann incredulously.

"I'm afraid so, Ann darling. Try not to hate me for it," Clarita answered.

"I couldn't hate you, angel, if I tried hard, and I'm not going to," Ann told her. "It's just that sometimes it seems to me the Cay is first in all our plans."

"Only in mine, dear," Clarita corrected her. "I admit it is a shameful thing to be willing to sacrifice someone you love for the sake of a scrap of land and the welfare of several hundred people. But now that the Cay has a very fine doctor and an excellent nurse to take over from Dr. John, there is no danger of anyone being sacrificed. I hope some day, darling, the Cay will mean as much to you and Tad and your children as it has always meant to me."

Ann bent and kissed the crumpled old cheek.

"It does now, angel," she said gently. "Only I'm just so almighty glad that David and Julia are staying, so I can stay, too. There's a lot of work for Tad and me to do, and we'll do it just as faithfully as if I had come back as a nurse."

"I'm sure you will, dear," Clarita told her. "Now bring Tad and let me congratulate him."

Ann flew to the wide door of glass opening on the terrace and called as she swung it open, "Oh, Tad, the grandest news! The Cay's going to have a doctor and a nurse!"

"I know what you're going to say, Clarita," he began.

"Do you, Tad?" There was a twinkle in her eyes.

"You're going to say she's got to go back to Blalock."

"And if I do?"

"Then I'm sorry. I've never fought you before, but right here and now I will." Tad's tone was even more belligerent. "She doesn't want to be a nurse. She wants to stay here on the Cay and marry me—"

"I know," said Clarita gently. "And I'm very happy about it."

Tad looked like a man who had taken a step in the dark and found there was no step here.

"You do? You are?" he stammered.

Clarita looked at Mary and smiled.

"It took us a long time to get our most cherished wish, Mary, didn't it?" she asked.

Mary looked at Tad, then at Clarita, and laughed.

"But it was worth waiting for, wasn't it?" she replied.

"Very much worth waiting for," Clarita answered. "All it took was a little separation to make them realize what you and I have felt for so long: that they were meant for each other."

Bewildered, afraid to accept the solution to a problem that had loomed so large in his thoughts, Tad asked, "What is all this? What's the mystery? Why are you all looking so smug?"

"Because we are so happy that you and Ann have finally waked up to the fact that you're in love with each other, of course," Clarita told him.

Tad studied her sharply as though suspicious of some hidden meaning in that.

"You're not going to insist she complete her training?" he demanded.

"Of course not," Clarita answered. "We're both delighted, Mary and I, that she is going to stay here and marry you."

Tad looked enormously relieved, and drew Ann into the tight circle of his arm while he watched Clarita warily.

"But you've insisted that the Cay had to have a registered nurse, and Ann was the only logical candidate," he pointed out.

"David and Julia are going to be married and stay here on the Cay permanently, and so I'm free to marry you and help you rebuild the Cay," Ann said eagerly. "Oh, Tad, isn't it wonderful?"

Tad looked from her beaming, radiant face to Clarita's smiling one and on to his mother's.

"Is that on the level?" he demanded. "They really are going to stay? They won't change their minds?"

"I'm sure they won't," Clarita answered. "You can both relax. I can't say I'm sorry I sent Ann away, because if I hadn't you two might never have realized that you are not brother and sister, but that you are genuinely in love. So it was best that she go away for a while."

Tad asked curiously, "Was that what you had in mind when you sent her?"

"Not entirely," Clarita admitted. "I hoped it would happen, but I couldn't be sure. And if it didn't, and she came back with her R.N. degree then there would no harm have been done. But I must confess I'm more than delighted at the way it's all turned out."

"Well, so am I," Tad answered, and looked down at Ann jealously. "But do you have any idea how close I came to losing her entirely?"

"Why, you did not!" Ann protested.

"The heck I didn't!" Tad's protest was just as heated. "Didn't you come back here all steamed up over the possibility of luring David into falling in love with you so that he'd want to stay on the Cay?"

Ann blushed. "Well, I didn't know then that he was in love with Julia. I thought he was available, so I went after him."

"You," Tad accused her sternly, "are a shameless young woman!"

"Ha!" said Ann, completely undisturbed. "Says you!"

"Says me," Tad answered her, and drew her toward the door that led out to the terrace. "There's a moon tonight, big and round and serene, as if it had never sent out a tidal wave to wash out a defenseless village. Let's go see it and decide if we can forgive it."

"Excuse us?" Ann laughed over his shoulder at Mary and Clarita.

"With pleasure," said Clarita firmly.

As the door closed behind the two young people, Mary and Clarita smiled at each other. Clarita put out her hand and closed it over Mary's.

"So now we don't need to worry about them any more, Mary," said Clarita softly. "Our generation—mine, rather—is finished here, and it's high time for the new generation to take over. And I couldn't be happier about the way it's all turned out."

"Nor could I," Mary answered, and did not try to deny the mist of tears that befogged her eyes. "My boy is a very lucky young man."

Clarita's smile was warmly tender. "No luckier than my girl," she answered. "And you and I are the luckiest of all."

"Aren't we just?"

Chapter Fifteen

Julia was seated in front of the dressing table brushing her hair when there was a light tap at the door and she called, "Come in."

The door opened, and Ann slipped in and stood leaning against the closed door, looking at Julia with eager eyes.

"Are you too tired for a little talk?" she asked.

Julia put down the hairbrush and turned about on the stool.

"Of course not," she answered. "Sit down and tell me all about it. You look as if something simply tremendous had happened."

"It has," Ann answered radiantly. "I'm not going back to Blalock."

"Oh?"

"I don't have to."

"But you were doing very well, Ann."

Ann laughed exultantly.

"Oh, I'll do much better here helping Tad rebuild the Cay," she answered. "And we owe our happiness to you and David. Oh, Julia, I'm so terribly grateful to you both."

"Now wait a minute," Julia protested, somewhat puzzled.

"When Clarita found you and David were willing to stay here permanently—" Ann began, and broke off to ask anxiously, "You are willing, aren't you?"

Julia laughed. "Well, not willing exactly. Let's say we are very eager to stay."

"Oh!" Ann's gasp was filled with unutterable delight. "Oh, Julia, I didn't dare dream that anything so wonderful would happen."

Julia's tone was touched with mockery. "You'd planned to marry David yourself and keep him here that way, hadn't you?"

Ann caught her breath and her eyes flew wide as a deep, abashed color flooded her face and her shamed eyes dropped away from Julia's mocking gaze.

"I didn't know you suspected."

"I did, almost from the first," Julia told her dryly. "After all, you weren't too subtle about it: inviting him down here and then including me in the invitation as a very obvious afterthought. At first I was tempted to go all haughty and refuse; but then I decided I didn't dare trust a man I'd had my eye on for three years to come alone to a place like this with a very devastating female who obviously had plans for him that didn't include me."

Ann said huskily, "You make me so ashamed."

Julia smiled. "You needn't be. You're by no means the first girl who's tried to snare David. But I was always around so I could fend them off. And I wasn't about to let him away from my protection."

Ann stared at her, round-eyed. "Do you hate me, Julia?" she asked.

"What a stupid question! Of course not." Julia's tone was quite sincere, her smile friendly. "Remember the old saw about 'All's fair in love and war'? Only you weren't in love with David, so I couldn't let you get away with trying to marry him. Now could I?"

"Well, no, of course not," Ann stammered, scarlet with confusion and embarrassment. "And I'm so glad, so terribly glad, you came, Julia. Honestly I am!"

"Well, thanks. So am I," Julia answered.

For a moment the two girls eyed each other, and then Ann said anxiously, "I think David would have been safe from my clutches, even if you hadn't come with him."

"Really?" Julia's tone frankly doubted that. "It was a chance I couldn't afford to take."

"Well, when I got back home and saw Tad again, I realized that after all, he was my man; not David."

Julia nodded, her eyes merrily mocking.

"But if I hadn't been along, you might not have discovered that," she pointed out.

"Well, maybe not," Ann admitted. "I did like David a lot."

"But you were not in love with him."

"Well, no. That day on the beach when you told me your plans for him—"

"That sounds as if I intended to manage the daylights out of him, Ann," Julia protested. "They were not my plans for him; my plans were just to trail along with him anywhere in the world he wanted to go, doing anything in the world he asked or expected of me. When he told me that he wanted to stay here and carry on Dr. John's research and was afraid I wouldn't want to—well, that was the moment when, for the first time, I could let him see all the way into my heart. And he let me see into his! And now we are here at the Cay permanently."

Ann asked after a fearful moment, "You don't think you'll get bored or homesick?"

"I could never be bored or homesick where David is," Julia told her with beautiful simplicity. "For wherever David is, that's home for me. I couldn't ever want anything else."

Ann glowed radiantly. "Well, you'll love it here once Tad and I get things straightened up. It'll be a beautiful place once more, and we'll have a lot of fun. You'll see."

Julia smiled at her. "Of course it will. And you and Tad will be as happy as David and I."

For a moment they could only smile at each other, and then Ann said huskily, "Welcome to the Cay, Julia dear, for always. It's your home now as much as it has always been mine. And you'll love it as much as I do."

"Of course I will, because David will be here and I'll be his wife," Julia answered, her voice not quite steady. "And what girl could ask for anything more?"

"She'd be a fool if she did," Ann managed, and their unsteady laughter rang out as they fell into each other's arms.